UNDERNEATH THE MOON 2

DAN HOLT

Published by:

MAX HOLT MEDIA

UNDERNEATH THE MOON 2

Published by Max Holt Media
303 Cascabel Place, Mount Juliet, TN 37122
www.maxholtmedia.com

Disclaimer: This is a work of fiction. Names, characters, businesses, places, events, and incidents are either the products of the author's imagination or used in a fictitious manner. Any resemblance to actual persons, living or dead, or actual events is purely coincidental.

The author is totally responsible for the content and the editing of this work and Max Holt Media offers no warranty, expressed or implied, or assumes any legal liability or responsibility for the accuracy of any information contained herein. The author bears responsibility for obtaining permission to use any portion of this work that may be the intellectual property of another person or organization.

Other books by Dan Holt: SLEEP MODE,
                             UNDERNEATH THE MOON
                             KEEPSAKE

Coming soon: UNDERNEATH THE MOON 3

Cover Design: Max Holt Media & Eddie Holt

Cover art by: ID 49926608 © Rfischia | Dreamstime.com
(Earth and Moon)

ISBN 13: 978-1-944537-06-7

Acknowledgements

I want to thank all 5,600 of those who read and enjoyed my first book, Underneath The Moon, during its first seven months on the market. That book was recently released on AUDIBLE.COM as an Audio Book. This sequel will also be released on Audio.

The unexpected substantial fan-base in Australia has been very gratifying as well. Many of you have communicated your anticipation of this sequel. I appreciate your encouraging words as I continue to flesh out the journey that began in a trunk full of old NASA photographs.

I want to thank NASA and the many astronauts for inspiring me as I watched the space program unfold over the years and sat transfixed as the first footprints were made on the Moon.

My wife, Mary, continues to be my biggest fan and she provides wise counsel during the writing and editing process. Her patience still amazes me.

TABLE OF CONTENTS

Prologue

Professor Charles Liggins, anthropologist, watched the saucer-shaped spacecraft, Research One, approach the landing pad in Aurora, Illinois. The newly minted ship, piloted by a NASA astronaut, Colonel Marvin Andrews, and copiloted by its inventor, Frank Gordon of Chicago, was returning from a mission to the Moon where they had discovered a burial chamber containing hundreds of *giants* in suspended animation, humanoid in appearance. The extraordinary craft and its intrepid crew had undertaken the venture following an extensive search through NASA's archives of the Apollo program and its photographic records that revealed evidence of *artifacts* on the lunar surface. The discovery of the ancient humanoids, completely hidden from the Apollo astronauts during their brief landings on the Moon decades earlier with their limited equipment, was a happenstance of a buried vault viciously opened by a wayward meteor. Research One, decades later, with its much greater maneuvering ability had flown into the vault and into history.

The professor, in his many field trips and digs, had discovered minuscule bits of evidence of the giant's existence in the remote past. He'd studied many ancient writings referring to the same, including Biblical references; but this, the lunar discovery, was the proverbial *jackpot*; if these creatures were still alive.

Charles Liggins, Professor of Anthropology, University of Illinois, Des Moines, ironically was instrumental in the creation of the prototype of Research One. He had introduced a researcher, a discoverer of evidence of lunar artifacts, to an inventor, a colleague from college; one with a place to go, the other possessing the means.

Douglas Charles Hastings, the discoverer of the ancient ruins on the Moon, had spent three years digging into old photographs from the Apollo era and was ardently searching for a means to return to the lunar surface and investigate. Frank Gordon, owner of Gordon and Gordon Magnetics, had developed a new type of propulsion, still in the testing stage, that was patented as 'Magnetic Inertial Propulsion.'

The two's quest led to a machine with the capabilities to traverse the quarter-million miles to the Moon and investigate the suspected artifacts. On board the returning ship were samples of the same: glass, possessing the strength of steel; a black carbon-like material, very light but amazingly strong; black cubes, as yet unopened, housing the secret of antigravity; books, discovered in an underground room, written in some alien language; and mysterious crystalline rings discovered with the books.

But, most of all, on board the craft was an astronaut, launched during Apollo, secretly, and then marooned on the Moon, that found a way to put himself in suspended animation using the equipment left by the giants, eons earlier. When awakened, the Lt Colonel had suffered no ill effects. Also, the sleep-canister had been acquired and returned to Earth.

During the mission, during the discovery process, as the news of the 'finds' were radioed back to the ground crew, Charles had begun making important phone calls. Some on his call list, fellow anthropologists, upon learning of the fantastic discovery, also made key phone calls, and the news spread through the hallowed halls of government very quickly. The media was already present and covering the very newsy development.

A Congressional Hearing soon came about. Each crew member of the newly minted spacecraft was called to testify. Their likability, both with members of Congress and the public at large, soothed the wounds that Research One had opened. Upon the completion of crew member #6's testimony, Roger Stahls took the stand and made the plea:

"This crew, flying this craft, saved me from eternal imprisonment in a tomb. Let's all save those helpless giants who are also human or human-like beings from that same awful fate. That's what America and NASA are all about."

Government officials quickly seized the opportunity to heal some old wounds, the wounds that all governments experience in the annals of politics when temporarily falling out of favor with the citizenry and needing something to build unity again. Here, it surfaced as a twenty-four-foot saucer, housing an invention, a 'Made in America' invention, that made it more than just a fantasy. NASA was the medium and the federal government the muscle to enter this new world on behalf of the people.

ONE YEAR
LATER

Chapter 1

And there were giants in the Earth in those days....
Genesis 6:4

SINS OF THE PAST

General Tulles, commanding the classified Orion Research and Development Complex in the mountains of Nevada, listened as the Congressman droned on about the inhuman act of leaving Lt. Colonel Roger Stahls, an astronaut, stranded on the Moon to die. He finally stopped after carefully orchestrated dramatics and an exaggerated show of concern.

The general spoke: "Congressman, those people who, supposedly, arranged a classified launch from this base during the Apollo missions are long dead."

"Supposedly, General Tulles," the Congressman responded with exaggerated incredulity, "it's been verified, Sir; we have a thirty-five-year-old astronaut that was born sixty-one years ago."

The general may as well not have heard the last exchange. He continued: "When I got the news of the pending arrival of this spacecraft from an unauthorized excursion to the Moon, I sent an agent to locate the retired astronaut that...supposedly...left Stahls abandoned on the Moon. My agent found Allen Brewster, that's the astronaut that flew with Stahls, dead at his own hand. His television was tuned to the station that was broadcasting the news. So, Congressman, it appears that the guilty parties have already received justice." The Congressman leaned back in his chair and then looked at the Chairman.

The General added his favorite testimony: "Since I and my team have had the responsibility of defending this country in this special endeavor, we have always responded to any inquiry made through proper channels." The general, known for his brashness, spoke again with a hardened face.

"Congressman, I think the oversight committee assigned as liaison to this important facility had a habit of sweeping things under the rug, especially since they were responsible for distributing money. After a few years, they didn't need the rug anymore." The general sat down visibly showing distaste for the one thing he could not control.

The committee Chair, elected to Congress during Apollo, now mellowed with age and no longer excitable, cleared his throat and spoke in a deep resonant voice; one of his campaign gimmicks that contributed to his many re-elections.

"Gentlemen, we have much work to do. We need a new committee to assist the General with his work. And, an oversight committee to work with NASA and the civilian sector to evaluate the bounty brought back from the Moon by the team that pulled off this miraculous venture. We must move forward." The general's face softened. He glanced at the smooth-voiced spokesman, then back to the Chairman. The Chairman continued:

"General, NASA's going to develop a fleet of ships, equipped to return to the Moon, working with Mr. Gordon at his facility. Gordon and Gordon Magnetics has serviced many government contracts over the years and is considered a mainstay for the needs of the government. The federal government is funding the project. I understand that the *mother* ship will be some 600 feet in diameter. A virtual aircraft carrier for space flight, made possible by Mr. Gordon's infamous Rotor Pod. It's a new day for NASA and a new beginning for planet Earth's space activities.

"Your job, General will be to incorporate into this nation's defenses this new form of propulsion. We are living in a new world, gentlemen. We cannot hide on Earth's little *island of innocence* any longer. It kind of makes me wonder how all those good people that gather in those buildings with the steeples on top are taking all of this."

The general opened his mouth then closed it again. He had virtually unlimited power but he knew to leave that alone.

Chapter 2

SPACE REGULATORY AGENCY

Frank Gordon, owner of Gordon and Gordon Magnetics, stood on the tarmac behind his Aurora, Illinois facility; *Earth Base One*. He was watching the graders, bulldozers, and enormous dirt-hauling trucks work. They were moving tons of soil and leveling the field next door for a 1000-foot-by-1000-foot by four-foot-thick foundation of concrete to be poured.

He felt fresh and new. A team of NASA engineers was pouring over his bulbous notes on the development of Magnetic Inertial Propulsion. It was discovered that the Navy had been working on the same concept for several years and, ironically, were very close to a breakthrough. The Navy's motive; an underwater propulsion system that would be undetectable. There was a saying going around that Frank must be a sailor at heart.

Douglas Hastings and David Henson, computer programmers, the architects of Research One's system of control, were working with a NASA team to acquaint them with the Hastings/Henson system, *as it became known*, for control of the Mother Ship, the 600-foot diameter behemoth and its shuttlecrafts, the 24-foot saucers that would be hangared in the mother ship. These smaller ships would be the excursion crafts for the various study groups that were to be part of the ship's company on the return mission to the lunar surface. The shuttles, Research One and five duplicates, would be hangared on the second deck of *Discovery*, the name of the mother ship by public vote.

Also, they would develop two freight carriers, specially shaped and contoured for recovery of the artifacts, crates, and equipment encased inside the tunnel discovered by Research One's crew. They had to be like NASA's Super Guppy airplane, minus its wings. They must be roomy but fit into the stone tunnel as shown in the video recorded by Research One. The two freighters would transfer the giants from their locations on the Moon to the mother ship of the Armada. Also, when facilities were ready, the giants would be returned to Earth and to whatever fate awaited them.

Daniel Stubblefield, the telemetry expert and crew member on Research One, would Chair the team that would work out the telemetry for the Moon-bound Armada.

Isaac Henson, the ship's safety officer for Research One, Dave's father, returned home after many interviews, pictures, and testimonials, with his wife Thelma. His age and his wife's health becoming issues, he decided to retire; again.

Colonel Marvin Dean Andrews, Captain of Research One, retired NASA astronaut, now reinstated Astronaut and Management Fellow at NASA, would command the Armada on the return mission to the Moon. The Colonel was working on the ship's crew selection with mission planners.

The completion time for the Armada of ships for the mission was estimated at just over two years. His bridge crew was already picked, if they would accept it.

Earth Base One

"The first thing we are going to do is build a ship identical to Research One," Marvin said to the assembled group at Earth Base One. "That can be done in ninety days or so because the details have already been worked out and the suppliers are all prepped to supply the parts needed, still having their molds and jigs from the construction of Research One. Two ships will go on the mission this time."

"Same original crew going back to the Moon?" Al asked. Marvin glanced around at the group.

"I like the tried and true. However, Isaac has requested to bow out for personal reasons. He will school his replacements; two NASA astronauts with space shuttle experience, on the nuts and bolts of Research One's systems and procedures. They will be assuming his responsibility; the ship's atmosphere. One of them will be on each ship. Daniel will be on board and will have a colleague, a telemetry expert from NASA, man the other ship.

"Also, we've asked Karen Hastings and Jean Henson to join the crew. As most of you know, Karen's a linguist and Jean's a geologist. Roger has elected to sit this one out. He's got twenty-six years to catch up on and wants to spend some time with his daughter. He will be working with NASA personnel on these new technologies and materials we brought back from the Moon.

"Frank insisted that Michael's promises made to those who assisted in building Research One be honored. And now, those companies have some very lucrative contracts with the government for this project. Their various labs have the materials we brought home; NASA has the life support cylinder and the antigravity cubes we found.

"One of the most important things they need from the Moon is a sample of that gas, or whatever it is, that kept Roger alive, and is now keeping the giants alive, assuming they are still alive."

Chicago Linguistics Institute

Karen Hastings sat in front of a supercomputer at the Chicago Linguistics Institute with stacks of books all around her; books that were brought back from the Moon on the first mission. So far, she was unable to get any of the symbols to match an English word or phrase.

"Rosetta Stone," she said. "If I had any type of Rosetta Stone to give me some insight on how to proceed." Jean Henson nodded, leafing through one of the books again.

"Notice," she said, "these pages of symbols, all circles and triangles, can be read left to right, right to left, up and down, and even diagonally the way they are perfectly spaced on the page."

"Yeah," Karen said. "There's a key; we just have to find it. This language is very deep, ah, sophisticated. Notice that you can go several pages before you get a repeat of an identical group of symbols." Jean nodded. Karen continued, "When we get to the Moon we need to look for repeating patterns; anything repeating. Maybe there will be help there on trying to figure how they thought; about their thinking patterns. We are going to have a linguistics lab in Discovery so we can work on deciphering their language there, where it was written." Jean nodded again.

"Seeing where the writing is, might be a clue to what it says," Jean said. "Writing on a certain building, or writing on a door, and then seeing what's inside."

"That just might provide an answer," Karen agreed.

The White House

The White House received many calls from various heads of state seeking information about the momentous discovery on the Moon. They were seeking involvement and offering support. President Howell put them all off until more information was gathered by various experts, promising to communicate appropriately at a later date.

President Walter Howell leaned forward in his chair.

"Gentlemen, it's time for the Federal government to give birth once again. Our last child, the CIA, was born September 18, 1947. That creation followed an incident similar to this.

However, that entity has morphed into a very complex secret organization that's engrained into the intelligence community of the government. The CIA is not configured to handle this development. What's waiting on the Moon is much grander and will require an agency dedicated to it."

Chief of Staff Tillman leaned forward. "What did you have in mind, Mr. President?"

"I've called all of you here to create another government body. We need a designation for the entity and to outline its responsibilities and its powers. The new agency will have the responsibility of the newcomers, the giants, if we find they are alive. And I've got a feeling they are. Earth has been comfortably ignorant for a very long time."

"Sir," Robert Foley, appointed to his cabinet position in exchange for bowing out of the race and cementing Howell's re-election, said to the President with conviction, "Waking those giants here on Earth could prove to be a disaster of epic proportions. Just suppose we bring a couple of them to Earth, awaken them, then wind up having to kill them."

"My God, Bob!" President Howell said.

"I think," Foley continued, "that we should install the necessary facilities on Discovery and have the crew awaken them, at least, one or two while they are still on the Moon." Stacy Gibson leaned forward and spoke:

"I agree with Mr. Foley, however, I don't think we should awaken them until we can talk to them; until we decipher their language."

"A linguistics lab will be on the ship," Tillman interjected.

"They're about to launch a second mission with two shuttles this time and there will be a linguist on board," President Howell said. "They have about two years to work on it before Discovery will be ready. Now, let's get to the matter of this new agency."

"Space Regulatory Agency," cited Tillman. "SRA, everything that comes to Earth from elsewhere is handled by this agency." There was perceptible nodding around the table.

"Okay, the SRA shall have Marshall Powers regarding all Off-Earth matters," the president resumed, "Agreed?" Consent was unanimous. "Okay, I'll submit it to Congress for approval. The agency would answer to the President and report to Congress on request."

Chapter 3

SHUTTLECRAFTS

Since the return of Research One from the Moon, following a few days of fanfare, the wheels had begun to turn, quickly going to full steam to prepare for a return to the Moon. Already, a pre-fab building had been subsidized and erected on the acreage behind Gordon and Gordon Magnetics in Chicago.

Parts and supplies had begun to flow into the facility for the assembly of the additional shuttlecrafts. In view of the mental conception of and the physical development thereof, Research One had morphed into a shuttlecraft; Shuttlecraft One, one of six that would be housed in and become a part of the spaceship known as Discovery.

Rotor pods were being produced at the rate of one a week from the three fabricating and tooling stations. Each, when completed, was promptly moved to a run-up and balancing lab, output test, final inspection, and then moved to a secure area for later installation.

The mother ship would be built at the Aurora facility. The sheer size of it required open-air construction on a reinforced concrete foundation. The entire area was completely enclosed in security fencing and patrolled by military personnel.

Shuttlecraft One had been flown to the Chicago facility for an alteration to its hull. The alternate ramp, measuring three-by-six feet, located just to the right of the windshield, was converted to allow a link-up with any of the other five sister shuttlecrafts and the two guppies while in space. All subsequent excursion ships would be so equipped. The crews of two ships, during a mission, could link up for conference purposes, personnel transfers, and, of course, rescue, should an emergency occur.

Additionally, four fold-down military style cloth cots were installed to improve sleeping arrangements on board.

Doug, Dave, Frank, and Marvin were at the facility to watch the final inspection team certify the first duplicate of Shuttlecraft One.

Doug looked at Frank. "What do we name this one?"

"Research One was unique," Frank began, "and will forever have her place in history. However, it's prudent that we move on and put her on duty as Shuttlecraft One, where she will serve with the same honor. This one now powering up will be Shuttlecraft Two, and the other four,

Shuttlecrafts Three through Six. We will give Discovery her rightful place; the center seat."

Bonneville Salt Flats, Utah

The completed Shuttlecraft Two sat at the edge of the forty-miles-square Bonneville Salt Flats for flight test. The government wished that the testing phase be done at the famous testing location as a catering gesture to the public at large and to spread the space activity closer to the folks on the West Coast. It was good public relations; large crowds were expected and were present for the test of the first minted duplicate of the famous Research One.

The crew, six in number; five of the original crew members, plus one NASA astronaut to replace the retiring Isaac Henson, stood at the ramp of their ship for pictures, then filed up the ramp and into the vessel. Shuttlecraft Two would be flown by Marvin Andrews, copiloted by Frank Gordon, safety officer, NASA astronaut James Larson, telemetry, Daniel Stubblefield, and two of the original computer experts; Douglas Hastings, computer control, and Dave Henson, computer safety systems. It would perform a test run under simulated emergency conditions; an exercise designed to put extreme stress on the rotor pod.

Marvin raised Research Two to 50 feet and hovered. He glanced at the crew to confirm the safety harnesses were in place and properly adjusted, and then stated:

"Engaging power at emergency acceleration." The crew, their body weight suddenly tripled, was pinned back into the cushions of their seats firmly. The terrain began passing under the ship 96 feet-per-second faster, every passing second. The firm pressure of the acceleration was constant as the velocity of the ship passed 300 mph; then 600 and climbing. The crew's attention was fixed on their readouts displaying the ship's status. Marvin watched the speed pass 1,000 mph, and then 1,500.

The hum of the rotor pod remained unchanged under the ever increasing power demand; the power required to push the wall of air in front of the ship faster and faster. The crewmembers were checking readouts, ever aware of the stress of such performance by a machine. Marvin glanced at the *new man*, astronaut James Larson, to see how he was handling the high performance of Shuttlecraft Two. He was fine. He knew about *G* forces. He had experienced 3*G*'s on the Space Shuttle. On that spacecraft, he had had to deal with severe vibration which comes with the use of rocketry. Here, Shuttlecraft Two delivered the same acceleration without vibration. Inertial propulsion was quiet and smooth; now 3,000 mph and climbing.

Marvin watched the speed readout pass 4,000, and then 4,500. They left the salt flats behind and the mountains loomed ahead. The AVS alarm sounded and the avoidance system engaged; the ship rose in altitude to clear the mountainous terrain. 5,000 and soon 6,000. When Marvin saw the speed register ,6000 his eyes went to the distance traveled; 76 miles, then to the elapsed time; 91 seconds. He pushed **CANCEL** on the controls. The computers quickly changed the performance to one quarter *G* deceleration. The ship slowly came to a stop and hovered.

"Any problems?" Marvin asked. Daniel raised his hand. "Colonel, all readouts are good. However, could we wait for a few minutes until my stomach gets here." Daniel grinned.

"We'll pick it up on the way back," Marvin said, turning the spacecraft around. He flipped open a cover exposing two buttons: **RET PO** and **CANCEL**, and ordered the craft to *return to the point of origin*.

Earth Base

With Shuttlecraft Two certified, she and Shuttlecraft One were transferred to Aurora and prepped for launch. Earth Base One had become a hub of space activities in view of the timely invention by the Chicago Company. The designation of Earth Base One was changed to simply '**Earth Base.**'

Doug, Dave, Ben, and Robert wrote and installed a sub-program into the computer control system to interlock the two ships together during the flight to the Moon. The ships would maintain proximity to each other while following the telemetry flight path. They would maintain a distance of one hundred feet apart, both following a path fifty feet either side of the *telemetry strand of spider silk* connecting the Earth and the Moon. The highway to the Luna.

Mission #2

Shuttlecrafts One and Two sat on the tarmac behind Earth Base, ready for a mid-morning launch for a return to the Moon. This mission would seek samples of machines, chemicals, and especially the gas discovered in the lunar lab that was being used for suspended animation; a state of extended sleep. Special containers were developed to capture samples to be returned to Earth.

Further, one additional excursion pressure-suit monitoring system was incorporated into the ship's design. It was agreed by all that the tethered suit system would be used since these missions were more dangerous in and around ancient ruins. The attached tether, now four incorporated into each ship, was a communications conduit connecting each suited member and the intercom on board so that all suited members and onboard crew could communicate freely. The voice communications were automatically radioed to the sister ship and its intercom system. The tether was also a hundred-foot safety line. The ship's design allowed freedom of movement of the ship about the lunar surface, thereby the tethered astronauts could have access virtually anywhere an untethered one could go. Very old structures were inherently dangerous. It was agreed that two radio-linked pressure suits would be carried on each ship for emergency use only.

Launch Day

"Ladies and Gentlemen," President Howell said, pausing to wait for the cheering and clapping to sweep the crowd in response to his new-found popularity. The cheering began to subside after a few minutes, then from someone in the crowd: "Way to go Walter," set the cheering off again. Minutes later, Earth Base was quiet.

"Ladies and Gentlemen, today, planet Earth is at a new beginning. We are sending two ships to begin the process of rescuing possible survivors of an earlier civilization of our Solar System. We want to help them if we can. We want to find out as much about what happened as we can.

"We are sending four specialists on this mission; a linguist, a geologist, a metallurgist, and a scientist who is a specialist in exotic and inert gasses. He will capture and return to Earth some of the special gas that kept our astronaut alive for so many years. It seems that they, the giants of the Moon, suffered some catastrophe that ended their civilization. We need to know what happened for our own safety and welfare in the future. We wish these crews God speed. I will now turn the mic over to our NASA administrator to introduce the crews that are returning the Moon."

"Thank you, Mr. President," Winston Stone said, "I will announce the crew members of the mission and ask them to line up here so we can all see them and get some pictures." As the administrator called their names the crewmembers walked out onto the tarmac and lined up waving at the crowd. Hundreds of camera's flashed. Minutes later the crews boarded their respective ships and the ramps of both ships majestically closed in unison. They began a final systems check. Launch was imminent.

Frank Gordon, waiting for the launch countdown to begin, looked around at the newly commissioned Shuttlecraft Two. It was an exact duplicate of the familiar Shuttlecraft One, twenty-four feet in diameter, twelve feet high in the center, sloping down to six feet high at the sides. It was the same inside except for the absence of scuff marks, scratches, and minor blemishes, the rewards of experience, that were now a part of the original Shuttlecraft One.

It had the six-seat arrangement facing a thick reinforced lead acrylic windshield, the same material utilized for years on the Space Shuttle. It was eighteen-by-twenty-four feet in size, just as the original. Shuttlecraft One had performed flawlessly during the gallant flight to the lunar surface, its built-in safety systems protecting the crew on a number of occasions, and returning them all, plus one soul, safely to the Earth. There was no reason this ship would not do the same. Frank had monitored its construction through all the steps; something he just *had* to do.

Marvin's voice came from the ship's intercom and the loudspeakers set up for the attending public: "Three minutes until launch." He did a final systems check.

"Systems check complete," Marvin announced, "counting from five; launch on zero."

"Aye, Captain," Frank responded for the sake of the crowd, positioning his hand over the **POWER** button. Amid an amazing moment of silence, Marvin's voice mesmerized the crowd.

"Five, four, three, two, one, Zero." The two ships left the tarmac instantly within a split second of each other. The computers quickly synchronized the acceleration and the reconnaissance mission was underway.

Karen and Jean, sitting side by side, both sporting new haircuts, hair cut short for training in the spacesuits for the mission a month before launch, looked through the bottom windshield and watched the tarmac and the Aurora facility drop away as the ship accelerated straight up. Many in the crowd were waving bye, a spontaneous gesture, watching the ships quickly get smaller and smaller. Karen and Jean watched the upturned faces grow smaller then group into a spot in their field of vision.

Soon, Earth Base was no longer distinguishable except for the thousand-foot-square apron upon which the mother ship, Discovery, would soon begin to take shape. They both looked toward Shuttlecraft Two, Shuttlecraft One's sister ship, keeping pace with them. Frank, piloting her, was looking at Shuttlecraft One. Frank waved. Karen and Jean waved back. Each found comfort in the other's presence. Seconds later the first *intersection* on the highway to the Moon was reached and there was a gentle nudge and the ship cambered to the left a few degrees. They glanced at Shuttlecraft Two; she was doing the same thing. The computer guidance had just established a new *Up* and *Down*.

The ships were accelerating at a constant $1G$ giving Karen and Jean's body mass the same value as the gravity of Mother Earth. Karen's 120 and Jean's 135 pounds were maintained, compliments of the Rotor Pod. There would be a 30-second interruption during the mid-point reverse of power; a small price to pay for a vastly improved mode of transport.

"All crewmembers," Marvin said to his crew and to Shuttlecraft Two via radio, "make sure your safety harnesses are properly adjusted. We are passing through the satellite belts and orbiting debris-field of planet Earth at a tremendous velocity. If we encounter any space junk, the AVS, avoidance system will make the necessary moves to avoid a collision. Some of them could be quite strong. We may not encounter any; there's lots of room in space. However," he concluded, "there are lots of junk, too."

Chapter 4

ASSIGNMENT

Thomas Thornton dialed the number attached to his new assignment. Following the death of Allen Brewster, Thornton was instructed to contact the only living member remaining of the original team assigned to the Apollo era secret mission. He was to get his marching orders from him. Following the third ring, he heard the seasoned agent on the other end.

"Mason."

Thornton waited for a few seconds but there was nothing but the one word. "Mr. Paul Mason of the CIA?"

"This has got to be Thornton. Tell me, have you got your CIA T-shirt on?"

"Sir?"

"Never mind. When will you be in town?"

"I'm at the airport, Mr. Mason. Sir, Allen Brewster is dead. Did you know that?"

"I don't want to talk on the phone. Get a cab to my office." Mason hung up the phone.

Paul Mason, fellow agent, colleague, and friend of Allen Brewster had suffered a tragic auto accident years earlier that left him paralyzed in both legs. Allen Brewster was the last pro-active agent on the assignment but his colleague, Paul, a variable steam roller despite his severe injury, maintained a daily vigil of work, records, and rapport with Allen and the quest. Now Allen's 'orphaned' young agent was assigned to him to use as he saw fit.

Paul Mason saw fit to recruit Thornton away from the CIA, as he, himself, had decided to leave the agency for some serious money from across the water. The KGB had seen this happenstance as an opportunity to get inside some knowledge paths and perhaps some of the bounty discovered on the Moon. Mason was about to tender his notice of retirement and was about to arrange some useful arms and legs in the young Thornton.

On Lunar Trajectory

Frank scanned the read-outs from the rotor pod again, a habit he'd developed that mandated he check every ten to fifteen minutes. Then his eyes found Shuttlecraft One, a hundred feet away, through the massive acrylic windshield. She was in lock-step with Shuttlecraft Two. Frank pushed the ship-to-ship control. "Colonel, what's your power readout?"

Marvin glanced at the console. "Nine-point-eight-six percent."

"I've got nine-point-nine-one percent," Frank responded. "We're heavier than you." Frank turned to his trip computer and brought up a formula then ran some numbers. "Colonel, we are carrying just over 154 pounds more weight than you."

Marvin glanced at Karen and Jean. "Frank, I'm carrying two women."

Karen and Jean looked up at Marvin then at each other.

Marvin continued: "Their combined weight is 255; your two specialists, Garner, and Roland, weigh 381 pounds. That's a difference of 128 pounds. The rest...you're carrying the Transponder."

"That's right," Frank said. "It's a little over 26 pounds."

"Frank, you're a methodical man," Marvin said. "A good thing," he added.

"Colonel," Frank said, "I don't think we should charge Karen and Jean full price."

"Oh?" Marvin played along.

Frank paused a moment. Karen and Jean looked at each other again.

"I've done some figuring," Frank continued in a serious tone, "and it doesn't take as much energy to accelerate them at 1G as it does the rest of the crew. They should get a discount; say 20%."

"Okay," Marvin said equally as serious, "I'll knock off 20%...let's see zero minus 20% equals...zero. Done." Jean and Karen were staring at him; Marvin grinned.

Frank glanced around at Shuttlecraft Two's crew and noticed Steven Garner, the 'gas man' staring straight at the console and not moving at all. He appeared to be deep in thought.

"Steven," Frank said breaking the silence of an otherwise quiet ship. Garner reacted with a start then looked at Frank. "Sir?"

"You okay?"

Garner took a breath and exhaled slowly. "I was...ah...just thinking about when we get there."

"It'll be fine," Frank said. "It will take a little while to get used to being so light on your feet, but, you'll be okay. One thing, at the half-way point you will be weightless for thirty seconds while the ship rotates for the reversal of power. Think you can handle that?"

"Yes, Sir, I don't think something like that will bother me very much."

"A suggestion," Frank said, "look straight ahead, breath normally, and count one through thirty. It worked for me."

"I'll remember that, Sir."

In an obscure neighborhood

A cab entered the half-Moon driveway of an elaborate brick home on a beautifully landscaped half-acre corner lot. Thornton got out and paid the driver and watched him drive away, then approached the front entrance. To his left, he saw a sidewalk leading from of the driveway and around the side of the house. At the base of the wall of the house was a white marble sign with gold letters: OFFICE. He followed the sign, turned the back corner of the house and followed the walk to a heavy entrance door and knocked.

"It's open," came from inside. Thornton pushed the door open and entered the office. Mason came from the connected house into the office steering his power chair behind his massive desk and indicating a chair for Thornton.

"You're cripple!?" Thornton said, and then checked his mouth.

Paul did not react. "No—inconvenienced."

"I'm sorry, Sir," Thornton said awkwardly.

Paul didn't even look up. "Don't worry about it. What are you called?"

"Sir?"

"What name do you go by; do you like Tom, Thomas, Thornton?"

Thornton shrugged his shoulders. "Just not TeeTee."

"I heard about that. A couple of agents started that and wound up making some medical claims, thanks to you."

The ex-marine set his jaw: "I didn't like it."

"I don't blame you." Paul changed the subject.

"Brewster's death. I had been expecting it for some time. When my car accident took me from his side, he began to come apart at the seams. Paranoia began to take hold of him. Then he was caught off guard with the saucer business and really looked bad. It was enough to push him over the edge."

"He fired me and I was the one that found that saucer first."

"I know, Thornton. He called me. He knew you were right; he thought he was teaching you a lesson. And maybe he did. But, you can forget that. This assignment is essentially over."

Thornton nodded. Mason studied Thornton's face momentarily. "I have an assignment that you are quite qualified for if you're interested. The CIA has nothing to do with it."

Thornton raised his eyebrows and shifted in his chair.

Mason continued: "I have retired from the CIA since all this business came about regarding the discoveries on the Moon. I have something else going on now. Over the years, I've met lots of people from lots of places. I'm working for the KGB now."

"What!" Thornton exclaimed.

Mason continued smoothly: "I need a good secret agent. You will tender your resignation to the CIA and join me. Let them think you're upset about the way you were treated or whatever; I don't care."

Thornton looked confused and dubious at the same time. "I've always wanted to be an agent. Brewster messed things up for me."

"How does a quarter mil a year sound?"

"Dollars!?"

Mason nodded. "I don't know the figure in Rubles." Mason opened his pencil drawer and picked up a letter.

"I've got your letter of resignation ready if you are interested. It'll go through smoothly."

The intrigue began to crawl up Thornton's spine; perhaps this is what he's really looking for. He nodded. "I'm in."

Mason handed him the letter and a pen. "From now on, its eyes open, mouth closed.

"I understand, Sir."

"Thornton, what I'm about to say to you doesn't leave this room. You know, I'm sure, that there are two ships on their way to the Moon right now." Thornton nodded. "These crews," Paul continued, "are going to retrieve a sample of the gas that kept that astronaut alive for twenty-six years and kept him perfectly healthy. Well, we have someone on Shuttlecraft Two." Thornton sat straight up in his chair. "An agent!"

"No, he's a scientist; a real one. He's a specialist in rare and exotic gasses. He's considered a genius by the scientific community. Needless to say, he's above suspicion; the perfect choice to get what we want.

"How did you get..."

"He has a nasty little problem that no one has discovered—so far." Thornton straightened in anticipation.

"Gambling," Paul continued. "He can't resist. When we discovered he had been selected for the reconnaissance mission we had some of our operatives arrange for him to run up nearly a hundred thousand dollars in gambling debt, then lean on him. He began to panic. We outlined our needs in exchange for paying off his gambling debt. He puts a sealed container of the gas from the Moon, the sleeping stuff, in our hands, and we deposit in his bank account one million dollars and make it look like a casino win."

"What do I do first?" Thornton said leaning forward.

Paul opened his pencil drawer, picked up an envelope and handed it to Thornton. "Everything you need to know is in here. Go to the enclosed address and contact Colonel Hamilton and let him know you're available and how to reach you. Give him the enclosed directive."

"Yes, Sir," Thornton responded getting to his feet.

Mason handed him a card. "This is your contact number for me. Stay in touch. Understood?"

"Yes, Sir. I need a cab."

"Waiting for you out front."

Chapter 5

THE MISSION

The morning show host introduced Colonel Roger Stahls and his daughter Renee. Colonel Stahls, promoted to full Colonel on national TV by the President and awarded a handsome check for twenty-six years back pay, smiled and waved, as per Renee's whispered instructions, at the audience.

"Colonel Stahls," the host began, "we have all read your incredible story of survival, when you were marooned on the Moon, in the papers and magazines. How did you feel when you woke up and saw the crew of Research One standing around you?"

Roger glanced at Renee then back to the host. "The first thing that popped into my mind was: *"wow, it didn't take them long to come and get me."* But when I saw their faces the first thing I said was: "boy, am I glad to see you guys."

"I imagine you were, Colonel. Were you aware of anything, maybe like dreaming, while you were asleep?"

"No. Nothing. I remember closing the cylinder, flipping the sealing latches, opening the valve on the last tank of oxygen that I had. I waited for it to fill the cylinder then I took off my spacesuit and turned on the cylinder with the control in the corner; it was a light beam; you just pass your hand through it. An eerie greenish gas began flowing into the cylinder. I felt so helpless. I turned on my side, pulled my knees up to my chest and hugged them. The next thing I remember is seeing the crew of Research One looking down at me. They...were...beautiful." Applause erupted in the audience for minutes, some standing and cheering. The host waited for the audience to settle down and then resumed.

"I imagine they were a welcome sight, Colonel. One other thing that lots of folks wonder about. When you walked down that ramp at Earth Base and saw your daughter running into your arms, did you notice her age?"

"When I saw her ponytail bouncing from shoulder to shoulder I knew it was her. I did see that her face wasn't sixteen anymore, but when I hugged her and then looked into her eyes, they were still sixteen and waiting for me to come home." Roger paused to regain his voice. "I was a little late." The crowd erupted again.

Earth Base

Al Billington, NASA Staffing and Administration, retired, part of Technical Research Association's ground crew, sat at the radio console of Earth Base. He turned from the TV monitor and activated the radio link to the spacecraft.

Shuttlecraft One, this is Al, come in."

"Go ahead, Al," Marvin said.

"Colonel, we just received confirmation. Shuttlecraft One's original crew is beautiful."

"What was that?"

"Roger and Renee are on TV again."

"Oh," Marvin responded. *They do have a story that's literally out of this world."*

Isaac Henson, sitting in with Al on this one: "Colonel, how was the mid-point turnaround?"

"Okay," Marvin said. *"Nobody panicked. No wrestling matches."*

Isaac chuckled. "What's first upon your arrival on the Moon?"

"According to NASA's new boss, Winston Stone, our first priority is collecting some of the chemicals, mainly a sample of the gas used in putting the giants in suspended animation. And they want some of those bottles we saw with the amber colored liquid inside, the ones in the lab.

"When we enter the tunnel we'll set up the transponder NASA provided at the end of it so we will have a radio link with Earth while inside the cavern and lab."

"Colonel, it might be a good idea to stop at the big piling where the cubes; the antigravity things are, and pick up a couple of them just in case."

"On the agenda."

Shuttlecrafts One and Two hovered one hundred miles above the central-most crater of the Moon. Daniel and James disengaged the telemetry link, locking the two ships together, and then the telemetry program and switched the vessels to local control. Frank rotated Shuttlecraft Two ninety degrees and eased the ship over to within twenty feet of Shuttlecraft One.

Doug looked down at the giant eighteen-mile wide crater on the lunar surface and at the equilateral triangle distinctly visible inside it; a triangle he'd examined closely on the previous mission to the Moon. Three huge light-gathering tubes were mounted on enormous pilings, so constructed to gather laser energy beamed from Earth eons ago to melt millions of tons of lunar sand into glass for the construction of a wonderful city and a protective dome over it. He activated the radio, as the designated spokesman for the mission, and notified the dignitaries down on Earth of their arrival.

Marvin and Frank began their descent. Both crews were a buzz of questions and answers, observations of things not noticed last time here, and awed at some of the bits and pieces that passed by the huge windshield as the descent continued. In just over an hour, touchdown was accomplished. The two ships sat in the giant concave surface facing each other; the two-miles-by-two-miles, twenty-foot deep mold that was used in antiquity to melt tons of sand into panes of glass for the, now shattered, dome. Marvin activated the ship-to-ship to do his duty.

"Gentlemen and Ladies, I don't have to tell you that what we are about to do is serious business. We are in a very hostile environment where mistakes can be deadly. Every move you make must be sanctioned. All excursions will be in tethered suits because of the hazardous area we are exploring. If anyone has his or her tether removed for some reason, to perhaps reach something important that is out of the tethers reach, that person must be in sight of another suited member of the crew at all times. Report any and everything significant; we cannot read each other's minds. Remember, you are in low gravity, one-sixth of Earth's. Move slowly and carefully until you have time to adjust.

"Okay," Marvin concluded. "The first thing we are going to do is go to that piling," Marvin pointed toward the edge of the crater to their left about half a mile away. "There's a stash of the antigravity devices stored in that piling there. We want to pick up four of them in case we need them. We discovered last time we were here that those glass cylinders are very heavy. They must be made of a very dense glass formula. The antigravity cubes will enable us to lift them."

Marvin signaled to Frank and lifted off the surface and traversed the distance to the support piling. He positioned his shuttle near the open door of the charcoal colored structure and hovered. Without a smooth area to land, Marvin, when the excursion team was ready to exit, would open the main doors and position the exit ramp, touching the lunar sand. Frank positioned his shuttle fifty feet away in an observation position to explain to the new members of his crew the excursion step-by-step as it happened.

"Doug, you, Karen, and Jean suit up and go inside and get four of the cubes and bring them on board," Marvin said. "Karen can check for inscriptions anywhere and Jean can examine the architecture," Marvin added.

Karen and Jean joined Doug at the storage area at the top of the rotor pod and retrieved their suits for the excursion. Their two pressure suits were equipped with a camera cable locked to the upper left arm and linked electronically to the audio system in the suit. Karen and Jean could depress a button on the camera and voice record pertinent information relating to the image being photographed.

With the three crewmembers fully in the suits and checked out they entered the airlock and were sealed inside. Ben activated the pumps for evacuating the atmosphere. Moments later, the gauges read zero.

"You okay?" Ben asked. Karen and Jean both nodded.

"We're ready for exit." Marvin activated the opening of the main doors. They slowly opened like a giant mouth and they were looking at the airless lunar landscape and the enormous circular piling with the ten-foot wide fifty-foot high door-opening facing the ship. Doug picked up a marine lantern and then walked down the ramp and bounced lightly onto the lunar surface. Karen and Jean followed, wobbling awkwardly getting used to their twenty pounds of weight in the lunar gravity. Karen leaned backward to check the top of the door opening for markings. She momentarily got overbalanced and took a step backward. Jean grabbed her arm and the two of them sat down on the ramp of the shuttlecraft. They helped each other get back on their feet.

"I was checking the top of the door for markings," Karen said.

"Don't worry about it," Doug said, "you are getting your sea legs, or, Moon legs. Get one of those marine lanterns attached to the wall of the exit ramp above your heads and follow me." Doug stepped through the opening into the piling and waited. Karen and Jean, carrying a lantern each, entered behind him and turned on their lights. The three beams of light crisscrossed each other with the illuminated circles rippling over the black shapes stacked neatly in the enclosure.

"My God," Jean said sweeping the structure toward the other side with the beam of light, "there's a lot of debris in here."

The light reflected only the objects that were in the direct circle emanating from the lantern. Karen moved out into the room several steps and then turned and studied the internal doorframe, slowly tracing its full height and width. On the left, relative to entering the structure, her light stopped half way down the doorframe.

"Look!" Karen said with excitement. "There're markings with an arrow pointing at the crates; the cubes!" Karen moved closer to the grouping of circles and triangles then handed the lantern to Jean and grasped her attached camera. Jean held the light steady while Karen took several exposures.

"These are our first markings with evidence of what they're referring to." Karen got her lantern back and began searching the rest of the interior.

Marvin spoke into the system: "Doug, how many of the cubes would you say are in there, altogether?"

Doug swept the room several times. "I'm going to guess about two hundred. They're stacked to the ceiling."

"Okay, bring four of them and we'll head for the tunnel."

Chapter 6

A SMILE

Shuttlecrafts One and Two approached the tunnel. Marvin activated the ship-to-ship. "Frank, follow me in. I'll move well into the tunnel so you can bring Shuttlecraft Two in as well. She's carrying the transponder so you need to be close to the opening of the tunnel. Have Dave, Steven, and Dwayne suit up to exit. Dave can plant the transponder for communications, then join the others. I'll send out Doug, Karen, and Jean."

The shuttle crews looked upward at the blue and white world, Earth, a quarter-million miles overhead, then down toward the bottom of the crater. Marvin began the descent. Frank followed. Marvin, following a general inspection of the three hundred feet wide and seventy feet high tunnel opening, moved Shuttlecraft One into the middle of the hundred feet wide aisle of the hallway, rotated her to face the containers and touched down. He turned on the exterior search light and aimed it down the hallway for the benefit of the new crewmembers.

The designated excursion crews were busily getting into the spacesuits and then being cleared with a final check by the safety officer. Each member found their suit a familiar piece of equipment, having spent hours familiarizing and training for this very event. Karen was eager to check the containers outside for writing, anything that might shed light on the context of their written language. So far, the symbols in the many books she had examined were a mystery. Maybe today....

"Is everyone ready for depressurization?" Marvin inquired. "Ready, ready, ready," came from the communication system.

Ben engaged the equipment and watched his charges as the atmosphere gauges crept toward zero. They announced ready for exit. Marvin activated the ramp opening. Doug heard the faint whining of the mechanism and the solid thump of the ramp on the stone floor. He marched down the ramp then turned and waited for Karen and Jean. They slowly baby-stepped down the incline, gradually getting more stable on their feet, then stepped onto the stone floor. The trio made their way around the ship to the front then looked up through the windshield at Marvin, Daniel, and Ben. They gave a thumbs up and smiled. Karen and Jean responded. Doug waved then turned toward the glass containers.

Shuttlecraft Two's excursion crew; Dave, Steven, and Dwayne appeared in front of their ship, then joined Marvin's crew adjacent to the containers.

"Everyone standby," Marvin instructed. "Wait where you are until Dave and Doug deploy the transponder and we check it." Dave, carrying the battery powered signal booster, made his way to the edge of the opening of the tunnel. He placed the base on the floor, swung the eighteen-inch dish, mounted on an extension arm, out into the chasm, looking for a clear signal trail to Earth, then turned the power switch to the ON position. The dish, in seek mode, quickly found and locked onto Earth.

"Okay, it's on." Marvin activated the radio: "Hello, Al, how do you read?" A few awkward seconds later the response came.

"Loud and clear." Marvin noticed the delay; the signal had to travel a total of half-a-million miles. Another reminder that they were far from home.

Karen headed for the closest container, the very one in which Doug had made his historic discovery months earlier. She wanted to see the fabled giant for herself. She approached his container and leaned over the top and looked inside. Jean was at her shoulder.

"Oh my God, he's huge!" Karen exclaimed.

"Look at that nose!" Jean said. "I've seen something like it...the *Moai* on Easter Island. The giant statues that were carved out of volcanic rock.

I took a field trip there in college. His face looks similar to those statues."

"Makes you wonder," Karen responded. "Those statues were carved about the same size as this guy." Karen and Jean were studying the face at length. Doug and Dave began examining the crate around the base looking for a feeder line supplying the gas to the container.

"Here's something," Doug said. "It looks like a square cover over something at the foot of the crate next to the base. Doug wiped the dust from the six-inch square block then tried to pull it free. It would not move. Dave positioned himself then kicked the box-shaped cover with the toe of his boot. The cover popped off revealing a two-inch diameter pipe coming out of the floor and entering the container. About two inches from it there was a T-shaped pin sticking out of the pipe. Doug and Dave looked at each other then turned and signaled Marvin through the ship's windshield.

"Colonel," Doug said, "I believe we have found the supply line and a valve that will turn off the system in this container."

Marvin got to his feet. "Standby, Doug, I'm coming out there. We need to know if that valve works." Marvin glanced at Frank.

"Go ahead, Colonel," Frank said. "I'll watch the ships."

Marvin suited up and processed outside, then made his way to the foot of the container. He carefully inspected the valve and nodded. He paused a moment then took a breath. "This might be a little bit of a chance, but we need to know if this system is actually working. Let's shut it off and see if there's any change. We can turn it back on immediately if there's any indication of a change in the environment inside where he is." Marvin paused again. "Everybody agree?" There was silence for a few moments.

"Colonel," Frank said from the pilot's chair of Shuttlecraft Two, "sooner or later, we will have to know."

"Okay," Marvin said. "Karen, Jean, Dave, watch the giant's face carefully. Doug, you back me up here on turning this valve. If we turn off the life support and he gets in trouble, we will have to get it turned back on." Doug nodded. Marvin checked to see that everybody was in position. He grasped the T-handle and exerted pressure clockwise. It didn't move. He re-positioned his gloved hand and exerted pressure counter-clockwise. The valve smoothly turned 90 degrees and stopped.

"Okay," Marvin reported, "it's off."

Karen, Jean, and Dave stared at the giants face. Thirty seconds went by, still no reaction, a minute, still quiet, then at one minute and twenty seconds there was a barely perceptible flicker of his eyelids then, a moment later, the eyes opened. Jean gasped. The giant's pupils narrowed to the incoming light then his eyes turned and focused on Karen's face.

"He's waking up!" Karen shouted. "He looked at me; he saw me!" Marvin quickly turned the valve clockwise, returning it to the original position. The giant blinked once then changed his focus to Jean's face. Jean smiled. The corners of the giant's mouth formed a half smile then it faded; his head settled back to center and his eyes slowly closed. All movement ceased.

The White House

"Now we know," President Walter Howell said to his cabinet. "Apparently, the giants on the Moon are the turn-of-a-valve away from being back in business."

"Question; what is their business?" Carl Vinton, Secretary of Defense offered. "We've got to know before we bring them here to Earth."

"Carl, pick a team, a security team, send them to NASA for training, and get them ready to be on Discovery when she launches."

"Will do, Mr. President."

"They must be able to communicate with the giants and determine their motivations," President Howell concluded. "They must also be so equipped

and trained to stop any threat that might surface."
His Chief of Staff spoke up:

"There's been speculation from the scientists that they may not be able to come to Earth. Their bodies may not handle the gravity. It's six times stronger than the Moon."

"That may be true," Foley said. "It depends on how long they have been on the Moon when they were put to sleep. If they are fully adapted to lunar gravity, Earth's gravity would keep them flat on their backs."

"All speculation," The president said. "They may have a physiology that easily handles just about any gravity. It's obvious, we are going to have to be able to communicate with them before we bring them here."

"If they can't come to Earth," the defense secretary said, "they will be back sleeping in their glass incubators a good while longer."

The Lunar Tunnel

Karen watched the giant's face for a long moment. The stillness of his countenance seemed unreal. This giant had reacted to a facial expression; a smile; displayed by her friend, Jean. Karen was thinking, *"They may not be all that different from mankind. The size, though; why would they be about seven times our size?*

"The scientists would wrestle with that for some time. Or maybe the giants could explain; when we are able to talk to them. Generally, higher gravity, smaller creature; larger creature, lower gravity. Our size relative to the value of Earth's gravity could be unique; perhaps we should be much larger based on the gravity formula. I'd be interesting to know the average lifespan of the giants. Maybe the giants have always lived on the Moons of the planets. We must figure out how to read their language."

Karen, on one knee, spotted a symbol etched into the T-handle the Colonel had turned off and then back on moments ago. It looked like a circle interlocking with two triangles. She caught the camera that was cable-locked to her left upper arm, aimed it and took a picture of the valve and then activated the audio and noted its location. She stood and looked around for Jean. She was taking pictures of the crates and the giants inside.

Marvin summoned the crews back to their respective ships to progress farther into the tunnel. The dignitaries back home wanted a count of the giants to begin assessing the problem of housing and feeding them if all went well and they were actually brought to Earth to live. Also, there were hopes that, further into the tunnel, an outlet could be located to get samples of the gas and other chemicals from the lab complex.

Chapter 7

THE MOON GAS

The two shuttles lifted off the stone floor and prepared to traverse the hallway deep into the lab that was waiting miles inside the eroded glass mountain. First on the agenda, count the giants.

"There're eight of them per row of glass containers," Daniel said. "They're about fifty feet long and there are twenty feet separating the rows. That's eight ever seventy feet into the tunnel. It was a couple of miles, if I remember right. That would be...about 1200 of them."

"1,200," Jean said, "enough for a small town on Earth."

"Giantsville," Karen said.

A smile played on Marvin's lips. He began lateral flight above the containers, deeper and deeper into the tunnel. He turned on Shuttlecraft One's lights as they distanced themselves from the tunnel opening. The two crews became mesmerized by the flashing young faces that, because of their size, seemed very close to the ship. Just over ten minutes later the containers stopped, leaving the floor bare. Marvin stopped and held; Frank, following behind, cruised to a stop.

"That's it," Daniel said, "1200 give or take, say twenty-four."

Doug radioed Earth with the update and noted that they would now begin locating an opportunity to capture samples of the mysterious gas that was performing a miracle; the miracle of keeping the giants asleep indefinitely without degradation.

"This gas," Marvin began, "there would have to be a tremendous reserve to last for thousands of years for so many 'users' and not run out. There must be cubic miles of it stored underground somewhere."

"It looks like Earth's scientists are booked for the next hundred years or so to figure out all this stuff," Daniel said.

Frank and Marvin positioned the ships facing each other and each turned to its right, spreading the light pattern to include the full width of the hallway. The ships touched down.

Steven Garner walked down the ramp carrying two special containers designed to capture the chemical, now referred to by all that were following the mission as *Moon Gas*, and headed for the area where the glass containers stopped. The crew had surmised that the plumbing continues on. Perhaps built in and waiting for additional containers to be set up when the disaster happened and caught them; the giants, by surprise. He hoped to simply turn on a valve and fill his tanks. He tried to maintain a relaxed focused demeanor as he made his way across the stone floor of the tunnel. He checked to see if the others noticed that one of his containers was slightly smaller than the recently designed NASA version. Also, it had no markings. He glanced at his crewmates again. None were paying any attention to him. He began searching the floor near the ending of the containers.

Frank, sitting in the pilot's seat of Shuttlecraft Two, watched the excursion team make their way across the hallway. Garner caught his eye when he stopped and glanced at the explorers near him a couple of times. It was out-of-character behavior for a scientist. Why would he care if his fellow crewmates were watching him? Something clicked in Frank's brain. The way Garner was carrying the containers; as if he wished that one of them wasn't so visible. *That's it...*Frank thought. *The containers are not the same. One has no markings on it and it looks smaller than the one with NASA's logo on it.* Frank thought again about Garner, daydreaming, on the way to the Moon. He thought nothing of it at the time. But now... Frank looked at Marvin examining the end containers and checking the figures inside them. Frank again watched Garner for a few moments. He kept checking the location of his fellow crewmembers while searching for an available outlet.

Frank reached up and switched off all the com links except Marvin's and paused the radio link with Shuttlecraft One, then spoke into the system: "Colonel, I need to talk to you for a minute."

Marvin turned and faced the shuttlecraft and looked at Frank through the windshield.

Frank continued: "I have switched off all the com links except yours. Colonel, I believe we have a problem." Marvin studied Frank's face momentarily then glanced at the other suited members then back to Frank. "I'm coming in."

Marvin walked up the ramp into the airlock of Shuttlecraft Two. Frank closed the outer door; the thick soft surfaces formed an airtight seal around Marvin's tether. NASA astronaut Robert Wingate, Shuttlecraft Two's safety officer, pressurized the airlock and opened the inner door.

Marvin took off his helmet and addressed the two NASA personnel of Frank's crew, Robert Wingate, and James Larson: "You gentlemen are sworn to secrecy."

"Yes, Sir," the two men said in unison." Marvin looked at Frank expectantly.

"Colonel," Frank began, "I've got a bad feeling creeping up my spine about Garner; Steven Garner, our resident gas specialist." Marvin glanced out the windshield at the scientist, then back to Frank's face. The two astronauts got to their feet.

"Why. What happened?" Frank related his observations moments earlier; the absence of markings on one of the containers. The way he was carrying the unmarked one. The way he kept checking the crewmembers around him as if to see if they were watching him. Marvin studied Frank's face a moment. "Frank, the man's a famous scientist."

"I know, Marvin, I know. I just can't shake this feeling. There's one other thing."

Marvin raised his eyebrows.

Frank continued: "On the way to the Moon, just after we checked the power readouts, I noticed him staring at the console like he was somewhere else. I spoke to him and he jumped like getting caught at something. I didn't think much about it at the time; I thought maybe he was nervous about the mission. I'm telling you, Colonel, there's something."

Marvin looked out the windshield again and located Garner and watched him momentarily. He was middle-aged, rather frail of build as scientists usually are, and an authority in the scientific world. *"However,"* Marvin thought, *"Frank doesn't make idle accusations; quite the contrary, he gives everybody the benefit of the doubt."*

73

Marvin spoke, "I can't believe he's on this mission to sabotage it. That wouldn't make any sense. The discovery has already happened."

"He's on this mission to collect some of the Moon Gas," Frank interjected," and that's what he's...oh my God, he's got some of it sold!"

"The extra container!" Wingate shouted. James Larson, Daniel Stubblefield's friend, and fellow telemetry expert looked at Marvin.

"Colonel, what are we going to do?" Marvin faced the three crewmembers.

"Nothing—now. He can't get off the ship until we return to Earth. His can't do anything with that container until we return to Earth." Okay, gentlemen, I'm going back out."

"Sorry for the bombshell, Colonel," Frank said.

"Frank, you may have saved us from a real nightmare." Marvin raised his helmet to put it on. "Turn the com links back on. If anybody asked about a delay or something, tell them you were testing the system." Marvin put his helmet back on, paused then removed it again.

"Frank, when I ask you to check your power readout from Shuttlecraft One, I want you to land, send Garner and Roland out alone. After they are processed outside, turn off their com links so I can address the entire crew at one time without them hearing it."

Frank nodded. Again, Marvin donned his helmet and was processed outside. He returned to his previous location and checked more of the giant's containers then made his way over to Steven's side. Garner had located an outlet and was working with it; trying to get a square cover off to check underneath. Marvin gave him a thumbs up. "Found what you need?"

Garner took a breath. "Ah, yes, Sir."

"It looks like the same type of valve," Marvin said. "Stand back." Marvin positioned himself the same way Dave had done at the mouth of the tunnel and kicked the cover off the T-handle valve. The cover slid about ten feet across the stone floor then slowly came to a stop. Marvin extended his hand.

"Help yourself. Don't forget to shut it off." Garner eagerly took his smaller container and slid the open end over the two-inch pipe and cranked the 'collar' down snug around the end of the pipe, then opened a secondary collar type valve located on the neck of the container. He then grasped the T-handle and turned it counter-clockwise. Through the transparent container, he saw a faint greenish hue flow into it. Momentarily it stopped and swirled inside the container. He returned the T-handle to its original position, closed the secondary valve next to the volume in his container then opened the outer valve and removed the container then closed the primary valve. He repeated the process with the NASA container.

Dwayne Roland, the metallurgist, picked up the dislodged cover Marvin had removed from the plumbing, held it up. Marvin gave him a thumbs up; a *go ahead and take it*, gesture. The expert placed it in a drawstring pouch attached to his belt. Marvin surveyed the excursion team.

"Okay," he said, "shall we re-board and proceed to the lab complex and see what we can collect there?" The excursion team began making their way back to the ships to be processed inside.

The twin ships slowly entered the immense volume of blackness. The two sets of exterior lights probed the darkness to the extent of their candlepower, reaching only more darkness.

"Frank," Marvin said, "hold right here; I'll turn on the lights."

The new members of the reconnaissance crews looked at each other in puzzlement then looked at Frank and then their eyes followed Shuttlecraft One through the windshield.

Frank smiled. "Just watch."

Marvin slowly cruised toward the brown colored pad near the wall of the lab that he and the original crew had discovered accidently. When he reached an intersecting position of the incoming light shining on the pad, a circle of light appeared on the upper windshield of the spacecraft—the entire five-mile-by-five-mile laboratory was flooded with light. A couple of members gasped in reaction.

"Looks like they paid the light bill," Dave said.

Frank chuckled. Marvin moved Shuttlecraft One back to Frank's position. "Frank, follow me." He flew Shuttlecraft One slowly across the lab, intersected the far wall, then left until he reached the area where the original Research One had discovered Roger Stahls asleep in a ten-foot cylinder. Marvin hovered above the row of familiar units. The fourth one was missing off its base. Pieces of broken black pipe lay on the floor beside the cylinder base.

"Frank," Marvin said, "check your power readout, then land where we did to get Roger and let Garner and Roland go out and get some that gas from one of the other cylinders and Roland can pick up some of those pieces of pipe we broke."

"Roger, Colonel," Frank said. "Power readout is normal, heading for the landing area."

"Okay, Frank, I'm going to move Shuttlecraft One close to these larger cylinders so Karen and Jean can search for labeling."

"Roger that," Frank replied. Minutes later Frank's voice came over the intercom again.

"Okay, Colonel. Garner and Roland are outside and I've cut their com links." The crew of Shuttlecraft One all turned and studied Marvin's face. Dave stared at Frank. Frank gestured—wait.

"All crewmembers, this is Marvin. Frank has cut the com links of Garner and Roland, who are outside now, for the purpose of this conference. I feel that you should be informed. We, Frank and I, have reason to believe that Garner, the gas specialist, brought an extra container with him for collecting the Moon Gas and has it sold when he gets back to Earth. The crewmembers glanced at each other. Marvin continued: *We think he has agreed to deliver it to someone for, probably, a great deal of money. I felt you should know. Everyone act normally for now. I'll let you know if there are further developments. We don't think Roland is involved, however, we don't know that. He and Garner are friends. Keep quiet for now. We are counting on you. As soon as Garner has all his containers full of the special gas, we will be headed back to Earth. We'll be coming back to continue our research."* Marvin paused momentarily. "Okay, Frank, restore the com links to Garner and Roland."

"Oh my God!" Daniel exclaimed; "he can't do that. Think about what could be done with that stuff."

"Yeah!" Doug, Dave, Karen, and Jean echoed.

"He's not going to be able to go through with it," Marvin rejoined, "On our way back to Earth, I'll cut ship-to-ship and notify the authorities to meet us upon touchdown on Earth. Frank, I'll cut ship-to-ship right after the mid-point turnaround and set up things for when we land." Frank acknowledged.

"Okay, Frank, restore their com links."

"I'm about to restore communications with them," Frank said, "don't forget that they will be able to hear you. Okay, restoring com links, now." Frank flipped the switches back to ON. The intercom instantly came alive: "….hello, hello, can you hear me?"

"Yes, I hear you," Frank said. "Sorry, Roland, I was checking one of the circuits."

"Frank, we need some help to reach the incoming gas pipe on this cylinder."

"I'll send out Dave to help you."

Chapter 8

THE GAS

Allen Brewster Jr, twenty-two, sat on the grave of his father, the late Agent Allen Brewster, and wept quietly. His father was a great man, always working alone to maintain secrecy for special government projects. Government secrets are very important. Sometimes somebody would get too close and his father would have to take care of it. They finally made a mockery of him and drove him to his grave.

Allen Brewster had loved Allen Jr's mother, a black woman, his maid, when no one else did. He was good to her. He wouldn't let anybody hurt her and make fun of her. Allen Brewster had pistol-whipped a fat guy one time for laughing at her. Allen liked that, nobody should laugh at his mother. She had told Allen Jr: "Your father is a man for real; that's what you want to be like."

"I'll get them, Father; I'll get them good." Allen Jr. sat on the ground with his back against the headstone, his knees up, and his arms straight out resting on his knees. He clenched his fists so long and so hard that his knuckles were white despite his smooth olive toned skin.

"I'll get them."

New Orleans

Allen knocked on an apartment door one block off Bourbon Street and leaned against the wrought iron railing of the second-floor balcony and waited. Presently, a short, curly-haired man in his forties opened the door a crack and looked out. Allen spoke: "My father said you were a good friend."

"I'm a good friend to lots of people; who's your father?"

"Allen Brewster."

The man quickly pulled the chain off the door, opened it and pulled Allen inside. He then stuck his head out and looked both ways, and then closed the door and locked it. He walked around Allen, then looked up at his face. "You're the kid! Oh my God, Kid, you've done some serious growing. How long has it been?"

"Ten years, Mr. Ritchie, I was twelve."

"Just call me Ritchie. I heard about your father, Kid. Sorry he had to go that way. Must be tough."

"They made him do it; the people in that saucer."

"Tough break, Kid, really tough. Why did you come to see me? What can I do for you?"

"A fake I.D."

Ritchie stared at the six-foot-six, handsome olive-skinned son of one of his favorite people. A realization crept up his spine. "Look, Kid, I know your old man got a rough deal out of all this stuff that's going on now. Maybe you should just let it go. These people and the government are...."

"How much?" Allen interrupted, his jaw set.

Ritchie walked over to his apartment bar, poured a whiskey, downed it, and poured another. He pointed the neck of the bottle at Allen and raised his eyebrows. Allen shook his head.

"One time, Kid, no charge for your old man. If you get caught, I don't know you, understand?"

Allen nodded. Ritchie downed the second shot of whiskey and set the glass down and picked up a pad and pen. "Who do you want to be?"

"I want to get a job building the ships that are going to the Moon."

Ritchie dropped his pen; it hit his shoe and rolled several feet across the floor. He chased it down, picked it up, and turned to Allen. "Kid, you're crazy! You mess with one of them ships the Fed's will kill you! They got soldiers all around them, with guns."

Allen Jr's face was frozen with hate. "I can pay."

Ritchie locked eyes with Allen for a long moment. "I told you, Kid, no charge." Ritchie was silent for a few moments pacing slowly across the apartment floor. He turned and looked up again at the handsome young face. "You're going to need an all-American, average Joe's, name." Ritchie stepped over to his desk, pulled out a drawer and picked up a well-worn black notebook and leafed through it then stopped on a page.

"Christopher James Miller, everybody calls you Chris. That's who you are going to be. Give me a week. I'll have you a driver's license, social security card, and a high school diploma. I've got a list of high schools that have been closed and consolidated in the past few years. It will be one of them. You be bright enough to go there and look the small town over so you can answer simple questions about it."

Allen's face thawed momentarily; he smiled and nodded.

The Lunar Lab, on the Moon

Dave exited Shuttlecraft Two and helped hoist Garner into position to capture two more containers of Moon Gas from the smaller cylinder next to the base of Roger's cylinder. Then the three were processed back into the ship. Frank raised his ship back to the altitude of Shuttlecraft One and when the two ships were facing each other about twenty feet apart an impromptu conference began.

"Garner," Marvin said, "how many containers do you have left to fill?"

"There all full, Colonel," Garner replied.

"Okay," Marvin said, "We've got one more important stop to make then we will be heading back to Earth.

"The bottles of amber liquid," Doug said.

Marvin glanced at Doug. "Right. Doug, Robert, Daniel, and Dave, suit up while we fly to that area. Let's get them and then see if we can fly up the tunnel that Roger came down to get in here."

Marvin and Frank traversed the lab, heading for the corner that housed the multiple cages for the experimental apes and the bottles of amber fluid captured on video on Research One's maiden voyage. They were able to land the spacecraft either side of the row of home-water-heater-sized transparent bottles. Doug and Daniel exited Shuttlecraft One and climbed onto the bench supporting the containers. Dave and Robert climbed onto the other side of the long bench. The units were freestanding; no attachments to anything.

"What a break," Doug said, "we can just carry them into the ship and secure them." Daniel laid his hand on one.

"Remember how heavy Roger's cylinder was," he reminded Doug. Doug grasped the upper portion of the device and pushed on it. As expected, it didn't move. Daniel assisted and the two could move it with great effort.

"Let's not struggle with it," Daniel said and headed back to shuttle to get one of the antigravity cubes. He returned to the glass container, placed the cube against it and he and Doug pushed on the odd side. It locked itself to the container.

"I like these things," Doug said. "I wonder if they're set just for lunar gravity."

"Good point," Daniel said. "If they are, then on Earth they would reduce the weight of something that weighed 600 pounds to 100 pounds which would help. However, when you got to things really massive it would seem like it's not working."

Doug nodded. "We'll have to ask about that when the smart guys figure them out."

Daniel picked up the glass bottle of amber liquid and headed to the ship. He placed it in the air lock, then deactivated the cube and headed back for the second bottle. Soon, both were inside the shuttle and the crewmembers were processed back inside.

Marvin and Frank headed for the far wall and the exit tunnel. Marvin slowly descended in front of the tunnel opening; noting that its dimensions were a duplicate of the tunnel they had entered at the end of the complex. There, a meteor had opened the door for them. This tunnel was an entrance by design. He noticed the three sets of Moon buggy tracks; Brewster and Roger came in; Brewster went out and blasted off for Earth; Roger walked out, or probably ran out, then discovered he'd been marooned; Roger drove the Moon buggy back down the entrance—alone. That must have been a long lonely trip, knowing he had only eight to ten hours of oxygen left. The rest was history: a magical, wonderful, story of courage and survival.

Marvin began the ascent up the inclined entrance tunnel toward the surface of the Moon. Frank followed in Shuttle Two. The tunnel was a marvel of construction; the ship's company could see a tiny rectangle of light far in the distance. The tunnel was straight as an arrow.

Karen and Jean studied the walls as they slowly passed through the lights of the spacecraft. They were bare and very smooth. Minutes later Shuttlecraft One broke into bright sunlight. The crew noticeably took deep breaths as if moving into fresh air and sunlight, although there was no change in the breathed atmosphere. Daniel pointed to the right then swept his arm to the left, indicating the ruins of a surface neighborhood.

"Colonel," Jean said, "take us up a couple hundred feet so I can get a good picture of the foundations. I'll study them when we get back to

Earth." Marvin raised the ship and held. Frank eased up beside them. The crews studied the devastation below. It seemed a sad relic of something that was once utterly magnificent.

Daniel imagined the buildings complete, glistening in the subdued light coming through a protective dome and atmosphere captured by the sealed canopy over the city. Perhaps children had been flying short distances with homemade wings, or chasing each other, in the low lunar gravity. Cautioned by mom, 'no higher than fifty feet.' Daniel smiled at himself.

Jean took pictures the full width of the windshield. Marvin turned the ship and began the flight back to the central crater and the launch point for the return to Earth. Frank followed. Soon they were sitting side-by-side on the giant mold located in the central crater.

"Shall we go home," Marvin said. "We can sleep on the way. It's almost midnight on Earth. That will put us landing at about 6:00 a.m., counting the last hundred miles of free-flight." The vote was unanimous; sleep on the way. Daniel Stubblefield and James Larson loaded the telemetry programs according to the clocks declaration of the location of the Earth and the Moon relative to each other; then engaged the computers, which engaged the rotor pods for a five-hour traverse between the Moon and home.

The spaceships were underway. The crews folded down the cots of the two crafts, then lay down, speaking quietly with each other. Marvin and Doug took the first watch on Shuttlecraft One and Frank and Dave on Shuttlecraft Two. Moments later, the rotor pod humming the song of sleep in the quietness, the crews settled into sleep.

A quiet ship, a star-speckled void, and an eventful day became a nursery of thought. The, now-seasoned, voyagers glanced at each other.

"Doug," Marvin said quietly, "your discovery set this adventure in motion. It's almost as if it was ordained by fate."

"Maybe it was, Colonel," Doug said. "Twelve hundred citizens of an ancient, magnificent society, threatened with obliteration by their technical pursuits and saved from it by their technical achievements. We seem to be their hope and we haven't progressed near as much as they had."

"It would be nice if they spoke English," Marvin said.

"Yeah, it would. However, I've got a feeling it's a much deeper language. I've also got a feeling they made up English as part of their project in that lab. Karen will figure it out; she's pretty sharp."

Marvin nodded.

"When we take care of this business at hand, we'll get her and Jean back to the Moon and focus on that. They're not going to allow transport of the giants to Earth until we can communicate with them."

"Can't blame them," Doug said.

"No, I suppose not."

Frank and Dave in Shuttlecraft Two glanced at each other. They were hearing the restless sounds of Steven Garner, lying down with the rest of his shipmates, but finding rest, especially sleep, elusive. One who had loved the pursuit of science all his adult life found it difficult to engage in wrongdoing. He would be glad when he had delivered it and it was over. A million dollars; a casino win, they said it would be. He struggled to remain still and quiet.

'Twenty minutes to Zero-G transfer to deceleration phase,' the voice mode of the telemetry program announced.

Following the transfer to deceleration Marvin, having an ugly chore to tend to, made sure the ship-to-ship communications were off. He then radioed Earth with a request to talk to a special agent of the FBI. It was almost forty minutes when the dignitary answered the summons on the radio to Shuttlecraft One.

"Go ahead, Colonel," Special Agent Oliver Thurman said. Marvin outlined all that had happened with Garner and his extra gas cylinder. Franks observations and their suspicions. For the agent's benefit, Marvin explained every detail.

"Colonel, you're sure."

"Yeah, we're sure. I wish we were not and it turned out to be a mistake." The agent was silent for a moment.

"Me, too. Okay, I'll set things up to monitor Garner and find out who's trying to get their hands on this stuff."

When the two ships settled on the landing area of Earth Base, Colonel Stahls and his daughter Renee were standing on the tarmac. Marvin walked down the ramp straight to them and kissed Renee, then smiled at Roger and shook his hand.

"Saving her father's life got you off to a good start, Colonel," Roger said. "We won't need to do the 'what are your intentions thing'."

Marvin laughed.

Marvin looked up when James Garner, carrying his four cylinders of Moon gas, made his way to the waiting staff of his lab. He joined them and the group exited Earth Base and went to a van waiting outside. A team of two agents, assigned by Special Agent Thurman accompanied them. Garner inquired who they were. Thurman explained that NASA had asked for security for them in view of the important material they were carrying; security would be in place at his lab.

Agent Thomas Thornton, blending in with the early morning enthusiast welcoming the two shuttles back to Earth, observed the bottles of gas being placed in the van and the arrangements surrounding it. He, with newly-learned caution, casually made his exit and headed for a phone. Thornton related his observations to Paul Mason on his *hotline*. He was instructed to wait a few days then contact Garner privately concerning the delivery of the special Moon Gas. He would comply. The 'gas man' had already made contact and related the security arrangements by the FBI to Thornton and said that he needed more time. The special cylinder was *on ice*.

"Colonel," Roger said, "what's the next move while the main fleet is being completed?"

"We'll take a few days to evaluate and plan, then we are taking our linguists and geologist back to the Moon for further research. We've got to understand their language. That's now the priority. Karen is taking two more linguists from the institute. They are getting their medicals and orientation now. They want total ship time to locate inscriptions and labeling, everything we can find to work on this language."

"Colonel," Roger said, "while I was looking for oxygen, right after I was marooned, I saw some regular sized books in some of the big offices when I was searching them. They were the same as the pile of books we brought back."

Marvin focused on Roger's face. "Was there a machine there with the books about four-foot square that had a chute, like a mailbox chute, on it?"

"Yeah," Roger said. "How did you know that?"

Marvin looked around until he located Karen and Jean. He raised his arm and whistled. Many, including Karen and Jean, looked at him. He motioned for them to come over. They made their way through the scattered crowd. "Karen, Roger knows where there are additional regular sized books in the lab complex on the Moon."

Karen turned to Roger. "Talk to me."

"Like I told Marvin, when I was looking for oxygen I went in several of the huge offices to search them. In two or three of them there were shelves of books, regular sized."

"And a reading machine," Marvin added. Karen glanced at Marvin and then back to Roger.

"Those books won't be about the solar system; they are going to be about the business in the lab," Karen said with passion. "Roger...Colonel Stahls, I want you to return to the Moon with us. We have got to decipher this language."

Roger nodded, then added: "I am kinda' getting tired of the cameras and talk shows."

Karen turned to Marvin. "Set it up, Colonel; this is really important. This could be the break we need."

Two days later Marvin picked up the phone and dialed Special Agent Thurman. The agent picked up the phone on the second ring. "Agent Thurman, what's the latest on Garner and the gas? Were we right?"

"Don't know, yet. They have opened only one of the three cylinders and began testing. We..."

"Three? Oliver, there are four cylinders; we brought back four cylinders from the Moon. Three of them have the NASA logo on them. Then there's one smaller that's plain."

"You're sure!?"

"Frank and I watched Garner fill the small one. He filled it first."

"Oh, boy," the agent said. "Nothing has left the lab. We check everything in and out. No cylinder has left the lab. Let me get on it. I'm going to search the lab and find it."

Marvin hung up the phone, wondering who was trying to get their hands on the special gas.

Chapter 9

THE TEACHING MACHINE

Workforce Solutions - Chicago

Allen Brewster Jr; Christopher James Miller, Chris, sat with twenty-three other petitioners for jobs in the government employment center in Chicago, Illinois, waiting patiently for his name to be called. The only thing that mattered to 'Chris' was getting a job with access to the Armada, any part of it, that was taking shape at the Chicago facility and the Aurora location. He bested the other applicants on appearance, demeanor, stature, and motivation, all deliberately. He had to have a worker's access.

Even though he hadn't slept for two days, and had been sitting here for hours, his eyes were electric, his voice true and pure, and his motive unshaken. Finally, he heard his name called by a stout black woman. He was next for an interview. He arose out of his chair as one who was *ready to go.* The woman looked at the handsome face and the electric eyes.

"Christopher Miller?" she said.

Allen nodded. "Yes, ma'am, I'm glad you called my name. I been wanting to do something really important and this job is really important."

"Yes, it is," the young government clerk said," impressed with the enthusiasm, (and the good looks), of the applicant. Tell me about your experience."

"Well," Allen said with a warm smile, "I worked with my father at the airport servicing small planes, gassing them up and stuff. Then right out of high school I got a job over at Boulder as a mechanic's helper; he was an Airframe and Power Plant mechanic. We rebuilt airplane engines. He taught me a lot. I really need this job because my father passed away and my mother can't work no more."

"Well, we can start you with a crew that's assembling the smaller shuttlecrafts. You'll start out as a helper."

"Thank you so much, ma'am. I really appreciate it." The clerk picked up a stamp, opened an inkpad, set the stamp on it then stamped a paper and handed it to the 'new Christopher James Miller'. "Okay," she said, "Go through that door and have a seat. They will come and get you and take a picture for your badge." Allen gave her the smile she had just compromised herself to get, and then eagerly entered the waiting room. Ten minutes later a bald man with earrings dangling from both ears and rings on all eight fingers took his picture then waited for a machine to 'spit it out'. He picked up the plastic badge with a metal clip on top and the image of the new employee of Technical Research Association printed on it and handed it to 'Chris'. He was instructed to report for work at the Chicago location the following Monday and report to Carl Weathers.

Earth Base

Truck after truck pulled up to the unloading cranes on the thousand-foot square concrete foundation. Aluminum I-beams in sets of six, each with a predetermined curve in its length, were pouring into the Aurora location. The set of six, when assembled into a single beam would be 300 feet in length and would reach from the center of mass to the perimeter of the vessel.

There were twelve sets that would be evenly spaced around the enormous craft, forming the bottom of the giant saucer. The diameter would total 600 feet, as the beams would oppose each other, spaced thirty degrees apart around the circumference.

The same deliveries would be made later for the upper half of the craft. Until then, when the bottom 'bowl' was completed, there were hundreds of internal features, systems, and partitions to be installed. The drawings of the internal layout showed a special lab 100-by-100-by-50 feet high, adjacent to the enormous hangar bay. It would be Karen's and Jean's Giant's Interview Room. There were signs randomly placed around the construction project: **SAVE THE GIANTS**. Some wished that a couple of them were here to lift some of the partitions into place.

The stock of rotor pods was growing as the teams carefully assembled them and checked their performance. Shuttlecraft Three was completed and would soon be taken for the operational testing, again at the Bonneville Salt Flats. Many of the interested public considered themselves to have 'season tickets' to the testing event.

One would never tire of watching such exaggerated acceleration. The ship would begin movement forward, then seem to zoom away, grow tiny, then wink out, all in a matter of seconds. Just after it winked out the sonic boom would arrive, accenting the moment. *An adage circulated among the youths in attendance that the new ships had warp drive.* It would then reappear in about half an hour and majestically return to its starting point and delicately land on its three legs. The giant mouth would open, the crew would come out and then a team of technicians carrying scanning equipment would enter the craft. An hour later, they would reappear, the crew would re-enter and the saucer would then rise up and fly away. A *first* in an air show; the first that was not about air, but about a new force that replaced it as a lifting medium—inertia.

Marvin, Frank, Doug, and Dave, trained a testing crew, personnel from NASA, extensively on the handling of the shuttlecrafts being fabricated at Frank's Chicago facility. They were commissioned to take each craft, Shuttlecraft Three through Shuttlecraft Six, as they were completed, to the testing area, Bonneville, and put them through the rigorous routine established to certify each craft's performance. The crafts must show the ruggedness to handle emergencies.

Launch Preparations

Edgar Windom and Joyce Mitchell, linguists, stood in the ready room of Earth Base for the final preparations before boarding the twin ships; destination Moon. Karen Hastings had picked them from the august body of the Chicago Linguistics Institute for the all-important task of deciphering the language of the sleeping giants on the Moon. The two, eager to be involved in the challenging task, after passing a physical exam, were voluntarily subjected to training acquainting them with pressure suits, emergency procedures, and onboard equipment.

The two Shuttles sat on the tarmac, fully prepped, ready to return to the Moon and deal with the saga of the giants. Shuttlecraft One carried Marvin, Doug, Daniel, Karen, Jean, and Roger. Shuttlecraft Two carried Frank, Dave, James, Robert, Edgar, and Joyce. This mission was about language. The spectators were few as compared to the initial launch. Now, most were home watching the drama unfold on TV. A news anchor was dutifully giving the event its due for the sake of the viewership. Half of the show was *a good announcer.*

Marvin went through the readiness check, received the okay from the twin vessel and then began the countdown. Upon launch, the two ships began their journey to the Moon on a, now, well-worn highway.

"Oh, my God!" Joyce Mitchell exclaimed moments later from her seat on Shuttlecraft Two, "the curvature of the Earth. It makes you feel like you're living on a small world." Karen glanced through the windshield of Shuttlecraft One at the sister ship keeping pace with them and replied through the intercom.

"In about three hours the Earth and the Moon will appear the same size." Edgar Windom scanned across the windshield.

"What a magnificent view of the stars, it's... Suddenly, the two ships moved away from each other, in a strong lateral move, an additional hundred feet. An object, silvery in color and shaped like a propane tank, zipped by like a rifle shot. Instantly it was gone and the ships returned to their telemetry flight path.

"What was that!?" Edgar exclaimed readjusting his posture in his seat.

"Debris," Frank said. "Part of a growing junkyard circling the Earth. However, now we've finally taken the next step and we can begin to get that problem under control."

"In fact," Dave added, "that will quickly become a flourishing industry now that society has the means to approach it. Some entrepreneurs will take a ship like this, outfit it with grappling equipment, come up here and chase this junk down and take it back to Earth; the big stuff anyway. The small stuff they can simply change the orbit so it will enter the atmosphere and burn up."

The speed of the twin crafts had now passed into the realm of 'miles-per-second.' The miles sped by at a constantly increasing rate as the spaceships followed their telemetry produced instructions.

"Twenty minutes to Zero-G transfer to deceleration phase," was announced by the voice mode of the telemetry program.

The routine, now practiced several times, was followed perfectly. The program disengaged power.

"Ahhhh," Joyce voiced quietly.

"You okay?" Dave said. Joyce looked at Dave and nodded.

"I been going to the gym to tone up and lose some weight. But, I didn't want to lose it all!"

"Don't cancel your membership, the weight will be back shortly."

"I never thought I would welcome it."

Dave smiled.

The Moon

The shuttles entered the underground tunnel, now a familiar place and the focus point in America's new space activities. With the ships landed, Marvin addressed the crews.

"Frank, have Dave install a fresh battery in the transponder then let's introduce our new spacefarers to the giants." Daniel, Karen, Jean, and

Roger suited up in Shuttlecraft One. Dave, Edgar, and Joyce in Shuttlecraft Two. Dave and Roger went directly to the signal booster and changed the battery; then returned to the group who had gathered around the giant's transparent home of many centuries.

"Look at the size of those eyes," Joyce exclaimed.

"Yeah," Karen said. "Marvin paced off his height; he's about seven times our size."

"Those eyes have depth," Jean said. "It was weird looking him in the eye."

"I wonder what his voice will sound like," Edgar said.

Karen looked at Edgar. "That's a good question."

Daniel stared at the giant's face momentarily. "He's about seven times our size; so are his vocal chords and voice box. Imagine our voice as the smallest string on a guitar; his would be the largest; roughly. I'd say he would emit sounds about an octave below us." All the group were looking at Daniel's face.

"It's a guess," Daniel added. Roger stepped over to the next container and looked inside for a moment then returned to the group and looked inside again.

"Karen," he said, "I think I've found something." Karen looked up.

"Have you noticed the small lettering on the collar of his burial robe?" Karen quickly positioned herself at Roger's elbow. He pointed. "Look closely at the robe where it comes to a 'V' on the chest. There's a symbol on each side of the 'V'."

"A triangle," Karen said.

"Now go look at hers," Roger said pointing at the next crate.

Karen hurried over to it. "Circles!" she shouted. "Male and Female! Now we are getting somewhere." The excursion crew quickly checked all the containers within reach of their tethers; all were the same—circles for females and triangle for males.

"That's Spanish-like in language base," Karen said. "The Spanish language has many words that are gender sensitive; example: the word for offspring is the same for both male and female; ending in 'o' it's a male, ending in an 'a' it's a female. Spanish is the second most-spoken language on planet Earth behind Chinese. Ladies and gentlemen we are going to figure this out." Karen looked at Marvin through the windshield.

"Colonel," she said jubilantly, "let's go find more samples of lettering and labeling; we'll solve this language problem."

Marvin smiled and motioned for the crews to board the ship and get underway.

The two ships made their way slowly through the depths of the tunnel. When they entered the large chamber again; it lay in darkness.

"The lighting must time out and turn itself off," Dave said.

"Guys," Roger said, "when we drove the moon buggy in here the lights just came on. At first, we thought that somebody was in here."

"There must be switches down on the floor in the halls or something," Marvin said.

"Yeah," Doug said. "That is something we will have to check out."

Marvin headed for the 'light switch.' The complex was, once again, flooded with light. He steered for the aisle where the lunar rover vehicle and Roger's letter were found by the crew on the first daring mission to the Moon. That would have been his starting place on his search for oxygen soon after being marooned. The, now ancient, moon buggy is another item that would be returned to Earth when the necessary equipment was available and would be cherished in a museum along with many other new and rare finds.

"Okay," Roger said, "I came in from that way; you can see the tracks, then got up on that desk and started writing the note to Julie. When I went looking for O2, I continued down this aisle to the end and turned right. Before I got to the next aisle there was a big office on the left of the hallway.

That's where I saw the first rack of books and that machine the Colonel mentioned."

Marvin steered Shuttlecraft One according to Roger's instructions. Frank maintained sufficient altitude to have a visual vantage point above the partitions.

"There it is," Roger said, pointing.

Marvin landed the ship in the middle of the fifty-foot-wide hallway and Karen, Jean, Roger, and Doug suited up to investigate. When cleared for exit the team walked through the ten-by-fifty-foot doorway into the larger office.

"The books are in a bookcase on the desk," Roger said.

Doug, Karen, and Jean leaned back and surveyed the desktop eighteen feet above the floor.

"Roger," Doug said, "how did you get up there?"

"I jumped up to the bottom drawer handle, then jumped to the chair seat, to the chair arm, and onto the desktop. It took several tries. I fell back to the floor a couple of times. It's a wonder I didn't damage my pressure suit."

"You can thank the low gravity," Doug said studying the 'route' Roger described.

"We have the advantage of help,' Karen said. "Doug, you and Roger pick me up to shoulder height and simply toss me onto the chair seat. I'll wrap my tether around the chair arm and the three of you can climb up it." Doug and Roger looked at each other, then said in unison:

"Okay." Karen positioned herself beside the chair. Jean pulled extra slack in her tether. Doug and Roger grasped her lower legs and easily lifted her to shoulder height.

"On three," Doug said. He counted down and the two men tossed Karen, like a javelin, onto the chair. Karen went up and over the side and the chair seat and landed in the middle of its width. She got to her feet, stepped over to the edge, reached up and wrapped her tether around the chair arm twice, then held on to it. Doug, Jean, and Roger quickly climbed up it.

With about nine feet to go, Roger lifted Doug to where he was waist up above the desktop; he scrambled up on top then braced himself for the rest of the team to climb up.

Roger pointed. "Down at the end, by the machine."

Karen hurried across the desktop. She saw the relatively small shelf enclosure with twenty or so books in it and one that had been taken out and was lying open on the desk.

"I took it out," Roger said, "I wanted to see if I could read it."

Karen hurriedly picked up the book. The symbol groupings were also all circles and triangles, however, this book was formatted in question and answer form, or topic and discussion form. There was a distinct equal sign displayed between the groups of symbols. Karen looked at Jean standing at her elbow. "Is the equal sign standard throughout the galaxy?"

"Just might be."

Karen looked around at the large office and then up at Shuttlecraft Two hovering fifty feet above the dividing walls. Her eyes found the six-foot-high, four-foot-wide number '2' painted on her underbelly.

"Frank," Karen said.

"Yeah, Karen?" Frank responded.

"We need to know what this office was used for. Can you see any wires, pipes, tubes, or anything coming out of this office and connecting something in the lab complex?"

Frank responded by moving to a position directly above the office. "Standby. We'll take a look."

Frank, Dave, the two NASA astronauts, and the two linguists began scanning the top and walls of the office. Frank carefully circumnavigated all four walls. Directly behind the back wall of the huge office, there was a spread of five tubes, side-by-side, that led away in the direction of the cordoned off mile-square enclosures. Frank eased the ship forward and followed them.

"Karen," he said, "we are following a set of five tubes; standby." While Frank and crew were tracing the route of the tubes, the team in the office were closely examining the machine sitting on the giant desk.

Doug noticed a knob sticking up just behind the 'chute'. He grasped it and pulled. A lid, or cover, opened just a crack, so he lifted and tugged at the knob. A two-foot square cover opened up revealing a screen underneath. He folded the cover all the way open. The screen was one-by-two feet and just above it there was the familiar brown grid-like material with the black lines in it. A few seconds later, the screen lit up. Karen and Jean gasped and stared at it. Doug quickly picked up the book from the desktop and inserted it into the chute. Momentarily, the screen displayed a set of symbols, then scrolled several symbols, and then again displayed the original symbol followed by the scrolled symbols again. The alien device kept repeating the sequence.

"Karen," Frank said from Shuttlecraft Two. Karen broke her attention away from the machine's display screen.

"Yes, Frank, I'm here, go ahead."

"The five tubes from the office lead to the five enclosures, the mile-square ones where they kept the cavemen."

Karen acknowledged and then focused again on the screen. She described the machines display screen to the crew and then began reasoning out loud: "Why would the machine scroll the symbols in the book when you could simply read them out of the book? That doesn't make sense."

There was silence for a few moments. Then Marvin spoke up: "Maybe they are not from the book."

Karen looked around at Marvin through the windshield of the spacecraft. "When Doug put one of the books into the machine, it activated the activity on the screen."

"Maybe the machine, activated by the insertion of the book, is asking you what you want it to do. It may even be speaking and we can't hear it because the atmosphere is not in the lab now. Sound doesn't travel without atmosphere. Touch your helmet to the machine, you should get some of the vibration if it is indeed speaking." Karen, holding her breath, touched her helmet faceplate to the side wall of the machine. A faint tinny sound of spoken words filtered into her helmet and to her ears.

"It's talking!" she shouted. Jean, Doug, and Roger took turns touching the appliance and straining to hear some of the alien's language.

"Colonel—everybody," Karen said, "the machine is displaying a group of symbols, then scrolling five different individual symbols, then the main group again, then repeating it over and over."

"Five," Doug mulled, "five symbols, five enclosures, Karen, you know about languages; what are the five languages most spoken on Earth?"

Karen turned toward the ship. "Mandarin Chinese, Spanish, English, Arabic, and Hindi."

"I'll bet that's the five symbols you are seeing."

Chapter 10

SHUTTLECRAFT THREE

Chicago, IL

Carl Weathers, machine fabrication specialist, and his helper, 'Chris Miller', entered the final inspection bay of the Chicago facility following their mid-morning break to install the inspection plates on the rotor pod of Shuttlecraft Three. Carl had done the final inspection of the rotors and their respective magnets, certifying each one with his signature on his report.

The bell had sounded for a break and he and his helper took their coffee break, to return afterward and close the rotor pod, clearing the ship for testing. Following coffee, the two were cleared through the magnet test door, as usual, to ascertain that there were no Ferris objects on their persons before working with the rotor pod.

The powerful magnets installed in the rotor pod, neodymium rare earth magnets, high gauss, would rip a watch right off your wrist possibly causing serious injury. All tools were aluminum alloy, a nonferrous material.

They parked their mobile tool boxes on the ramp of the shuttle, then approached the rotor pod with the inspection plates lying on the floor by the ports they were to cover.

"Okay, Chris," Carl instructed, "let's start all these high tinsel fasteners in the inspection plates first."

"Yes, Sir," Chris responded and then began threading the bolts in the mounting holes of the plates.

Carl heard his name called from outside. He stepped to the ramp opening. A clerk in a white shirt and tie spoke again:

"Mr. Weathers, your wife is here and needs to talk to you for a minute; something about the school." Then the clerk disappeared. Carl turned to Chris: "Chris, I'll be right back."

"Yes, Sir." Chris waited for a few seconds, then looked out the ramp and saw that his boss had gone out the door. He quickly went to the rotor pod and stuck his head inside the open inspection port. He saw the eight 70-pound magnets mounted on a vertical aluminum alloy wheel. He could just reach the nearest magnet from his position. The magnet was secured by eight one-inch diameter bolts.

He quickly adjusted his spanner and removed six of them, leaving only two securing the heavy magnet. He placed the bolts in the bottom of his toolbox, placed a hand towel over them, and then put a couple of wrenches on top of the towel. He went back to threading the bolts in the plates as instructed. When he had all of them started, he lifted the plate into place and began wrenching the bolts into the rotor pod.

Carl stepped onto the ramp and entered the ship. "Ah, moving right along,"

'Chris' looked around and smiled. "Yes, Sir."

Carl picked up the other inspection plate, set it in place and then began tightening the bolts.

The Lunar Machine

"Colonel," Karen said looking at the windshield of Shuttlecraft One sitting in the middle of the hallway just outside the huge door of the alien office, "we've got to get this machine into the ship and take it back with us. With it, we can decipher this language in possibly a few weeks working with our computers at the institute."

"Doug," Marvin said, "check the weight; see if you can move it."

Doug slid his hand along the side of the machine to the back of it, wrapped his finger around the corner then pulled. The machine easily slid across the desk. "It's very light! What a break." He glanced at Marvin. "We've got to figure out how to get it to the floor from the top of this desk. It's almost twenty feet."

Marvin paused a moment, then got up from his seat and went to the back of his shuttle. Moments later he came back with two twenty-foot lengths of nylon rope taken from the tie downs over the parachute silk tarps. "Doug, you or Roger come to the ship and get these ropes. You can simply lower it to the floor with them."

Doug nodded and grabbed Roger's tether. Roger sat down on the edge of the desk and pushed himself off the side. Doug lowered him to the floor and then dropped his tether. Roger headed for the ship and returned with ropes in hand. He tossed them up to Doug and Karen and then climbed up Doug's tether.

They closed the cover on the machine and moved it to the edge of the desk and circled it with one of the ropes and tied it off. They then attached the other and pushed the machine off the side of the desk. They lowered it to the floor where Doug and Roger carried it to Shuttlecraft One and up inside the airlock.

"Roger," Karen said, "do you know of another one we can get?"

Roger looked at Karen and paused. "There was one close to the cylinder that I got in with my last oxygen bottle. I think it was just past the high dividing wall, on the left."

"Colonel," Karen said. "We may as well stay suited up in the airlock, and then get the second one before we process back into the ship."

"On our way," Marvin responded. Marvin lifted off and ascended to the height that afforded clearance of the partitions dividing the lab into office areas. He proceeded across the lab, again toward the small ten-foot cylinders. Upon arrival, he crossed the high wall and descended to floor-level and flew to the left of the connecting door.

Daniel pointed. "There it is."

The enclosure was identical in size. Marvin landed in front of its door.

Frank, in Shuttlecraft Two, was hovering above the dividers, in line with the tunnel where all the young giants were sleeping and the transponder was waiting in readiness. In the distance, he could see the tiny rectangle of light some two and a half miles away. Another reminder of the precision construction of this alien culture. A tunnel in solid rock, straight as an arrow.

The team; Karen, Jean, Doug, and Roger made their way around the ship and into the office. They quickly, with a now proven system, traversed the distance and were on the desk, ropes in hand. They secured the machine, with its library of books, and began the process of transporting everything to the spaceship. They had just placed the machine in the airlock and were being processed back into the atmosphere of the ship when Al's voice invaded the ships, calling from Earth Base.

"Go ahead, Al," Frank and Marvin responded at the same time. There was a moment of hesitation; then Al spoke:

"Frank, Colonel, I just got a call from the support team at the Bonneville test site. Shuttlecraft Three exploded on a test run." There was silence in both ships; the crews were riveted to the radio.

"Al," Frank said, "did you say that Shuttlecraft Three, the third excursion ship...exploded!?"

"Yes, Frank, it exploded. They were starting the high-performance 3G test-run when it happened. The engineer said it blew the top out of the ship. He said they had just raised the ship to 50 feet. When they engaged the rotor at 3G performance, within a second, it blew. The ship lunged forward, the top came out of it and it went to the ground at about a forty-five-degree angle and then skidded to a stop."

"Al," Marvin said, "what about the crew?"

"Two of the guys were injured; one had a piece of aluminum go through his foot; the other had a magnet fragment lodge in his hip. They're going to be okay."

"Lock down the area," Frank said, "I want to see every part of that ship."

"Already done; the National Guard has secured the area and set up generators and lighting."

"Colonel," Frank said, "we need to head back to Earth."

"We are closing the outer doors right now."

Chicago, IL

Carl Weathers, responsible for the final inspection of the Shuttlecraft Three, following his signing it over to the testing crew, had joined his wife at the high school for an after school conference. His son had gotten into a fight with one of his peers over a girl. The matter was handled delicately, as all matters regarding youth and academia, in a very time-consuming meeting, taking the better part of three hours. Following the exhausting conference, Carl took his wife to dinner at a local restaurant. Halfway through their meal a quiet buzz began passing from table to table. Carl signaled his waiter; he responded quickly.

"What's going on?" he quietly inquired.

"The new Shuttlecraft Three exploded."

"What!" Carl said loudly.

The waiter stepped back and repeated the news. "The new Shuttlecraft Three exploded, Sir, while they were testing it."

Carl and his wife got to their feet. "Check please," Carl ordered, "hurry." Carl drove home. He picked up the phone and called Al at Aurora wanting more detail on the shuttle's explosion. He explained that he did the final inspection before Shuttlecraft Three was released for the test. Al let him know that Shuttlecrafts One and Two would be arriving between nine and ten p.m., then Shuttlecraft Two would be continuing to Bonneville, if he wanted to drive over and join them. Carl said he'd be there. His wife quickly packed him an overnight bag and Carl made the trip to Aurora to await the two spacecraft.

Frank, sitting at the helm of Shuttlecraft Two as it accelerated toward planet Earth, looked around the ship, at the rotor pod, then back through the windshield. There was a solemn quietness inside the ship.

The first tragedy had invaded the world of a new, now patented, propulsion system. What happened had to be discovered. His mind kept going over the drawings of the internal workings of the rotor pod. He had personally inspected Research One, now Shuttlecraft One, they all had, and he had inspected all of the other new rotor pods. All had been right. All the parts were there; all where they belong. He would look at them again, and again, if necessary.

Marvin looked across at Shuttlecraft Two and then around at his craft. He got up, stepped over to the rotor pod and laid both hands, palms open, on the outer shell and placed his ear to the surface and listened. *Smooth, very smooth.* He patted the sphere, nodded, and returned to his seat.

His crewmates watched the episode, then resumed their posture, most looking at the starry sky as Shuttlecraft One traversed the miles back to where she was created. Marvin wondered what could have caused it; the explosion. Shuttlecraft One had easily outperformed two F-16s. He had a bad feeling creeping into his mind. *"Someone had gotten to Shuttlecraft Three's rotor pod. Who and Why?"*

Chapter 11

THE CRASH SCENE

The two returning shuttlecraft, sitting on the tarmac at Earth Base, were surrounded by the Illinois National Guard, put on alert when the third shuttle had exploded on a high-performance test. Shuttlecraft One's rotor was coasting down, having been shut off for the unloading of the special interpreting machines recovered on the Moon.

Shuttlecraft Two's rotor was still humming at the ready. She had another mission to embark on immediately. She would ferry Frank, Doug, Marvin, Dave, James, Daniel, and Carl, final inspector of the rotor pods, to the Utah testing area and the site of the mishap during the testing of Shuttlecraft Three.

Shuttlecraft Two lifted off the tarmac and headed due west. Frank selected 500 feet and 1,000 mph. The shuttle responded smoothly. Soon after midnight, they would be at the scene of the explosion to start looking for answers. This was the second day since the crew had slept. They would find it difficult until they had some answers; especially Frank. His machine, heralded as the next step in propulsion, had failed. He needed to see the wreckage. His mind went back to the construction of Research One by him and his colleagues. They had discovered that during their vigil of creating the ship, someone had entered it and activated some of the controls, probably trying to determine if the machine would actually function. They hadn't sabotaged anything, that time. But this time....

"Twenty miles," Marvin said, "disengaging power." Shuttlecraft Two decelerated and approached the downed craft ablaze with lights set up by the National Guard. Frank circled slowly above the ship using his search beacon to view the damage to the top of it. The machine was cambered toward the front. When the disintegration occurred the craft fell at a forty-five-degree angle. The tripod gear had automatically activated but did not have time to fully deploy. The impact had collapsed the front strut and the craft now leaned up on the other two with the windshield on the low side.

The jagged hole in the top of the saucer was about four feet wide. Down inside the rotor pod was a maze of ripped and torn metal. Frank hovered over the hole at length studying the damage.

Carl stared at the scene inside the rotor pod housing. It was a jumble of twisted beams and warped struts. It had taken enormous force to cause such total devastation. What could he have missed?

"Something came loose inside the rotor pod," Frank said, "and the rotating magnets collided with it, over and over, 5,000 times a minute; each magnet a seventy-pound hammer. We have to find every single part of this ship. Let's have teams search every square inch of ground for one mile on all sides of this vessel. The speed of that rotor could throw something that far."

Frank landed Shuttlecraft Two and made his way to the damaged Shuttlecraft Three. He singled out the pilot and copilot of the testing team. They weren't hurt by the explosion and were kept from injury during the hard landing by the safety harnesses. They explained the sequence of events again to Frank as they happened during the incident. He was introduced to Special Agents Wilson and Goodman of the FBI. They pulled Frank and Marvin aside.

"Does it look like an accident?"

"Don't know yet," Frank said. "We've got to examine all the parts. We'll search the area around the ship as soon as we have daylight."

The local commander of the National Guard approached the crew of the Shuttlecraft Two.

"Mr. Gordon, if you and your crew want to rest a while we have set up a tent for the duration of this investigation. You're welcome to make use of the cots. We'll be organizing a complete search of the surrounding area as soon as it's light in the morning." Frank glanced at the others and nodded.

"We may as well get a couple of hours if we can."

New Orleans

A block off Bourbon Street, Richie, sipping a whiskey, was watching the 10 p.m. news when the image of the damaged Shuttlecraft Three filled the TV screen. Ritchie sat straight up in his chair. The news media ran a video clip of the Shuttle, sitting motionless at 50 feet, then lunging forward, the top exploding, throwing debris high into the air, then the ship falling to the ground. The clip was repeated in slow motion. The scene went back to the Shuttle sitting at an odd angle, ablaze in lights.

"That stupid Kid!" he said. "Somehow, he did it!" Ritchie studied the scene on the screen for a moment. The blazing lights illuminating the craft and surrounding area of the white Bonneville Salt Flats had an eerie appearance.

"That's got Feds written all over it," he said then picked up the phone and dialed a number that was labeled in his brain under 'emergency.' The owner of B & B Transportation, Byron Baldwin's voice came on the line. Byron had as many names as he had fingers and toes, thanks to Ritchie. He also had a very lucrative arrangement to routinely launder money. Ritchie heard women giggling in the background.

"This is Ritchie; I need my apartment to be bare floor in two hours."

"You got it," came from the phone. Ritchie hung it up, opened his safe and picked up a packet and became someone else who lives somewhere else.

Allen Brewster Jr. sat in a squatting position at the end of his father's grave playing with some loose soil. He had been there for an hour, dry-eyed, staring at the headstone. He finally muttered in a strained weak raspy voice: "Father, I'm going to bed now. I'm really tired...."

Chapter 12

SABOTAGE

A ten-ton crane backed up to Shuttlecraft Three and positioned itself with the top sheave centered over the damaged spacecraft. The operator set the outriggers, then set the brakes on the behemoth to wait for clearance to lift and load the vessel on the waiting lowboy trailer. The heavy steel, multiple wheeled, truck trailer combination waited to back under the shuttle. The ship would be taken on the long journey, by highway, to Chicago, its birthplace, where it would be dismantled piece by piece and x-rayed.

The crew that had arrived from Aurora was inside the damaged ship probing into the rotor pod as much as possible to see if there might be a stray part or piece of debris that caused the catastrophic failure. So far, everything in there was supposed to be there. The National Guard had assembled fifty men and women to search the immediate area around the ship out to a mile, initially. So far several small pieces of metal, aluminum and magnet parts, heads of bolts and threaded bodies of fasteners had been found and turned in for inspection.

Then, mid-afternoon, the news, and the part came by jeep to the ship. The search team had found a complete magnet. Frank and Carl, followed by the rest of Shuttlecraft Two's crew, hurried over to the jeep to examine the find. The seventy-pound neodymium rare earth magnet was on the raised booster-seat of the jeep. There were two ball point pens, a wristwatch, and a money clip stuck to it. The money-clip still had the money in it, and under it, between the clip and the magnet was a patch of National Guard fatigue material. One of the guardsman's left front pocket had been ripped from his uniform while they were loading the magnet into the jeep.

"Don't try to get the items loose from it," Carl said. "We'll do that back at the company. We have special equipment for that." Frank and Carl examined the magnet closely for several minutes then the realization came. Frank pointed at the cluster of holes patterned on the magnet.

"Carl," he said. "Look at the holes closely. The two on the end have had the threads pulled out of them. The six in the middle are pristine, like new."

"Oh my God!" Carl said. "The bolts were removed before the failure!"

"You're sure they were in the magnet when you released the craft to the testing team?"

"Yes, Sir," Carl said, "they were there. I have a system I use for the final inspection. Each magnet is an assembly of nine parts; the magnet and eight one-inch, high tinsel bolts. I physically count each assembly then check it off on the inspection form then sign it. They were there."

"Okay," Frank said. "Between then and the moment the testing team engaged the rotor at 3*G*'s somebody gained access to the pod and removed those bolts. Apparently, a Quarter-*G* wasn't enough stress to break the two remaining bolts when they were flying out here to the test area.   The high-performance test made the problem show up. Gentlemen, those bolts could not have loosened themselves or drifted out; they are self-locking."

"That means we have a saboteur," Marvin said, "and he or she somehow managed access to the rotor pod long enough to remove those bolts."

"Where and how?" Dave said. The group was silent for a few moments.

"Carl," Frank said, "you were the last person in this ship before it was turned over to the testing crew?"

Carl nodded. "Me and my helper, Chris Miller." Frank thought for a moment.

"I can't see the testing crew sabotaging the ship then getting in it and making a high-performance run."

"Carl," Marvin said. "Maybe somebody got by you, somehow, did the deed, and disappeared."

"I don't think so."

Marvin thought for a moment. "Let's go backward through your day until we get to your inspection of Shuttlecraft Three."

Carl nodded. "Okay."

"You boarded Shuttlecraft Two in Aurora with us. Where were you before that?"

"I drove from home. Wanda, my wife, packed me an overnight bag and I drove straight to Aurora."

"Before that?"

"My wife and I were having dinner at a restaurant close to my son's school. That's where I got the news about the explosion. We had a conference at the school; my boy got in trouble. Blasted thing lasted almost three hours."

"You went from work to the school?"

"Yeah,"

"You must have gotten a call from the school at work."

"No, my wife came by the job and..." Carl fell silent.

"What?" Marvin said. Carl had a strained look on his face.

"The office sent someone to get me. I went to the front to talk to my wife. Chris was alone in Shuttlecraft Three, with the inspection plates off the rotor pod, for about fifteen minutes."

"Did you check it afterward?"

"No, I didn't think a thing about it. When I got back he already had the inspection plate mounted and was tightening the bolts. We buttoned it up and I signed it over to the pilot."

"Frank, that's got to be it," Marvin said, "it's the only opportunity to get those bolts removed and the plate back on undetected. Carl, tell us about this guy."

"He seemed a great guy. Eager to please; hard worker; great attitude."

"How long have you been working with him?" Frank inquired.

"He just started a few days ago but I was completely satisfied with his work."

"He could have set you up; eager to please until he gets an opportunity. We have to check him out."

Carl nodded. "Sorry, I let my guard down."

Frank summoned the FBI then related their fears to Special Agent Wilson. Carl suggested that the FBI search 'Chris Miller's' toolbox immediately. Each worker at Technical Research Association was issued a special set of tools for working with the powerful magnets of the rotor pod; the tools are the property of the company. Therefore, the company could grant access. Agent Wilson made a call to Chicago. Within two hours, two field agents in Chicago served a warrant on Technical Research

Association and cut the lock off the toolbox and searched it, finding six one-inch high tinsel aluminum bolts in the bottom drawer under a red shop towel.

Special Agent Wilson issued the order to find and arrest Christopher Miller.

"That's it," Frank said breathing a sigh of relief. Even though they had a ship destroyed beyond repair the drive was a solid dependable power plant. Frank looked at Carl.

"Check all the rest of the rotor pods. Assemble a team of three inspectors, yourself and two more. When the three of you can certify them, put a hermetic seal on each inspection plate."

"You got it," Carl said with finality.

"What's a hermetic seal?" Daniel said. Frank glanced at the destroyed shuttle.

"It's a metal band that will lock the inspection plate to the rotor pod; the only way to get the inspection plate off is to destroy the seal. You can't remove the plate, have access, and then replace it. And every seal has a unique number molded into it." Daniel nodded.

"Well, Gentlemen," Frank said. "We can head back to Chicago. Carl has a lot of work to do and we've got to generate another work order for a new Shuttlecraft Three."

Chapter 13

THE LANGUAGE MACHINE

Two months had gone by since Shuttlecraft Three's rotor pod had been sabotaged and subsequently exploded during testing. Marvin, Frank, Doug, Dave, Daniel, and Isaac on a volunteer basis, plus the new crewmembers; James Larson, Robert Wingate, and Benjamin Thorne were busy training new crews in the operation of the shuttlecrafts soon to be commissioned as part of the Armada.

Twenty-four trainees were selected from a pool of many applicants; fifteen men and nine women. The methodology was patterned after NASA's approach to training astronauts over the years. A large amount of classroom time was allotted for a thorough understanding of the new type of propulsion and especially the computer control of a very different vessel. That, followed by many hours of hands-on training in the craft's themselves, proved to be a daunting training program.

Karen, Jean, Edgar, and Joyce, set up the two 'reading machines' brought back from the Moon and began the tedious task of working with the alien language; the language of the giants. Moon language. There was banter among the teenagers to sign up, as soon as it was ready, to learn to speak 'Moon.'

Two more linguists from the institute joined in the group effort to discern the different languages apparently embedded in the alien machine; a teaching machine, by inference. The segments were played over and over and then compared to recorded Earth languages.

Then, breakthrough thinking, many times the result of group brainstorming, occurred and a laboring team member made the fateful suggestion.

"Let's bring in a linguist from each of those language-based countries." All eyes of the group went to the young face for a moment. Then Karen picked up the phone and called Winston Stone, the NASA administrator.

Two weeks later there was a caucus of language scientists pouring over the different utterances of the equipment recovered from the Moon. Two months later 'Moon' had been deciphered in a rudimentary form.

The computer could change *Moon* to English and English to *Moon*. Mankind would be able to speak across fifty thousand years to those who had been here before.

The government had closed Steven Garner's lab. The research efforts on the Moon gas were moved to NASA's Arden Research Center, along with two of the researcher/scientists from the Garner lab. The two dedicated scientists, oblivious of Garner's fiasco, had made some progress examining the 'Moon gas.' Testing with lab animals had revealed that the gas had regenerative effects at the cellular level. It seemed to repair moment by moment the effects of aging and suspend the cells need for activity. There was still no information about its origin or formula.

Agent Thurman had ordered a complete search of the Garner lab and had found the hidden smaller cylinder in the bottom filing cabinet drawer in Garner's private office. When confronted with the evidence, Garner had fallen apart. When the investigator set the discovered cylinder on Garner's desk, his face turned white, then he bent to the side and vomited on the floor and broke down with a complete confession. Ironically, he seemed relieved. The tension of clandestine behavior and rank wrongdoing was not his strong suit. The government, taking into account his many contributions to science and the public good, granted him a minimum sentence of eight years in federal prison; with the possibility of parole in four.

An Undisclosed Location

"They caught Garner," Thornton said sitting in Mason's office, "he's going to prison."

"Forget about him," Mason said. Thornton was visibly disturbed by the answer. Mason looked him in the eye.

"Thornton, you've got to learn when to let go. If you don't, you'll wind up planted beside your first boss. Besides, we have a lot more gambling debt to be collected. I think you will be a lot happier with these assignments." Thornton leaned back in his chair. From Agent to Operative to Collector then back to Agent by declaration, this world isn't what he thought it was; but he strangely liked it.

A several-month manhunt finally came together at an out-of-the-way apartment in the French Quarter, New Orleans. A young man, Allen Brewster Jr. got into a brawl at a club, was hauled downtown and fingerprinted during his arrest; then a fingerprint, on file at Technical Research Association for a Christopher Miller, came together to identify the hands that had sabotaged Shuttlecraft Three months earlier. Under interrogation, his motive was discovered. He was tried and convicted of sabotage and sentenced to twenty years in federal prison.

Chapter 14

BIG JOHN'S TAILOR

Returning to Earth Base following a training flight, Marvin ordered the formation of the six shuttlecrafts to *'all stop'* a quarter of a mile and five hundred feet altitude from the landing area. Ahead was the massive bulk of a near-finished Discovery, the mother ship. Marvin and his six crews, the twenty-four selected trainees, now trained and ready for the mission, never tired of viewing the marvel of technology that would change space flight and space research forever. The sheer size dwarfed Earth Base, the surrounding construction cranes, and cable trolleys suspended above the behemoth. The cars, vans, and trucks nearby looked like a hot-wheels collection scattered in a toy box.

Soon she will be ready.
Soon the world will change.

The construction would be finalized in thirty days. Then, there would be three months of internal and external inspection, system checks, rotor pod run-ups, emergency system dry-runs and checks, verifying every system redundant-times-

two, and a tug at every fixture just to know it's real and it's there.

Discovery's first time to break the bonds of Earth would be a test run of twelve inches; one foot, straight up. It would hover just off the support foundation for extensive testing of the all-important rotor pod assemblies, thirty of them, linked electronically. They must perform as a unit, flawlessly, to propel the giant mother ship without fail. The second test run would be straight up to the vacuum of space, laden with its six shuttle crafts, Shuttlecraft One through Shuttlecraft Six; and its two guppy-type freight movers. It would hover while the technicians, space suited, checked and verified the massive airlocks of the hangar bays and the personnel airlocks. All excursion ships would launch, circumnavigate, and reenter the mother ship and dock. Then Discovery, complete with shuttles and guppies, would fly to Bonneville for a demonstration for the public; a show that would draw thousands.

"All ahead, proceed to dock," Marvin ordered. The respective crews followed the established order of approach and landing procedure. After shutdown, the respective maintenance personnel entered each craft and checked hours-of-operation, bearing temperatures, distance traversed, and notes by the pilot, if any. All were logged to the respective craft. Each ship now had a history and a support team.

As Discovery neared completion so did the details of the Armada. The manifest, the bridge crew, and the entire ship's company had to be selected for the journey to the Moon and into history. Some two hundred and eight souls would staff Discovery on the initial voyage. Also, there were details concerning the most gripping aspect of Discovery's mission. The prudent handling of awakening a civilization of millenniums gone by. Winston Stone summoned Marvin and Frank to his office for a private conference.

"Marvin, Frank, we are going to need about two more cubic yards of the gas that is keeping the giants asleep. We are constructing a pressure tank to keep the pressure on the giant's glass case to transfer him to Discovery from the underground tunnel. We will fabricate it to fit over the tube supplying his gas, cut the unit loose from the supply then affix our unit and match the pressure.

We are sending a special saw; high rpm, diamond-toothed. It will cut the feeder pipe quickly so you will have time to restore his supply before he begins waking up. That will take care of him until the transfer is made. We will have a dead-end clamp to install on the severed tube that will read the pressure so we can set our unit."

Marvin nodded, appreciating the NASA style efficiency.

"Also," the administrator continued, "find out how the glass containers are opened. Do they have simple over-center type clamps like Colonel Stahl's canister?"

Marvin and Frank looked at each other. "We didn't see them if it does," Marvin said. "We'll check them out this trip and know for sure."

"Also, we feel it to be only prudent to be prepared to handle the giant we awaken should he, for some reason, get out of control and become a serious danger to the ship and all aboard. We will construct a unit to release it in volume that will put him to sleep again long enough to restrain him."

"Will do," Marvin said. "Also, we'll use this opportunity to take the pilots of the six newly-trained crews on the mission to give them the experience of having been there before the launch of Discovery."

Winston Stone nodded and stood. "Oh, by the way; Big John's Tailor wants his measurements."

"What?" Marvin responded, puzzled.

Winston Stone smiled. "We are fabricating pressure suits, three of them, for the giants just in case things go really well and they can actually show you guys around Moon City."

Frank smiled. "Okay, will do."

"Best guess, as close as you can," Winston added.

Marvin nodded, shook hands, and left.

Marvin informed the new shuttle pilots of their assignment and set the launch date at two days away. NASA delivered the bottles, larger than the originals, for capturing the needed agent. Shuttlecrafts One and Two were checked and prepped for the mission.

Daniel Stubblefield's crowning achievement was sitting in the communications lab at Earth Base. A mainframe computer programmed with the orbits of the Earth-Moon System. The colossus would create a telemetry program for launch to the Moon on any day, simply by entering the date requested. It set the launch for 6:21 am.

Marvin and Frank cleared each of their ships for launch, then Marvin did the customary countdown. The surge of $1G$ was there instantly followed by a faint nudge of synchronization of acceleration in each ship and the new pilots were into their first voyage to the Moon.

Marvin looked at the list: Jackson During, Lucas Wilbur, Joyce Hayden, Tim Woodward, Melissa Ryan, and Logan Oliver. In the group, he saw talent. They had trained diligently and were now good pilots.

Melissa Ryan, one of the new shuttle pilots, looking through the windshield of Shuttlecraft Two, watched an airliner just out of Chicago O'Hare, climbing to altitude, drop below the plain of view. She again noted the power of the machine which she had been trained to pilot. In the years to come, Chicago O'Hare would be the home and the stop-over place for many modes of transport vastly different than the machine she had just seen and very similar to the one she now occupied.

The new voyagers studied the heavens as the miles rolled by, although the ships were constantly getting faster and faster, the stars did not reflect any differently than they would have had the velocity been constant as during Apollo.

The vast 'lightyear' distances were too great. From the galactic core, the Earth and the Moon were virtually in the same place. The computer, the brain of the new form of transport, was the source of reality for the spacefarers. They must know it, understand it, and trust it.

The midpoint turnaround was assigned to the new pilots. The classroom time had paid off. The episode went well on both crafts, save a floating camera lens cover on the Shuttlecraft Two. It found the floor immediately when power was engaged for the deceleration phase of the journey. Gravity by acceleration is just as real as gravity by mass.

The Moon

The ships first visited the piling and the source of gravity cubes, proven to be the most useful tool on Luna. They obtained four more, then entered the tunnel. As usual, Shuttlecraft One first and Shuttlecraft Two following, positioned to service the transponder with a fresh battery. Having done so, Doug and Dave escorted the new voyagers to be introduced to 'Big John' as the admiring public had begun to refer to the giant that had smiled at an Earth woman.

The newly trained shuttle pilots gathered around Big John's container and viewed the giant head of the forty-foot tall citizen of the ancient solar system.

"I wonder what he was doing here on the Moon," Jackson said. "What was his job?"

"When we are ready and wake him up, we can ask him," Melissa said. The six new voyagers looked at the sea of glass containers in the stone tunnel in awe.

Marvin reached into the leg pocket of his suit. His hand came out of it with a cloth measuring tape. He handed it to Daniel. Daniel raised his eyebrows.

"Big John's Tailor want's his measurements," he said, smiling.

"You serious?"

"They are sending three pressure suits for the giants on Discovery just in case things go really well."

Daniel looked out the windshield at Big John's container and then at the tape. "I worked as a tailor when I was in college," Daniel said.

"I know, you told me several years ago."

Daniel suited up and made his way to and joined the group gathered around Big John. They turned and looked at him, and then at the tape in his hand. "We need Big John's measurements for a pressure suit just in case he makes the cut."

The new pilots looked at each other. Marvin explained as Daniel took the measurements and passed the information to the ship via the radio. Marvin watched Daniel finish the chore. "Okay, Doug, you and Dave see if you can determine how the crate is opened."

Daniel joined in the examination of the container for latches, handles, anything for access.

"Colonel," Doug said, "the lid is separate. You can see that it sets on top of the box, but I don't see any latches. Maybe it's fused together."

"How would they get out?" Frank said.

Marvin glanced down the hallway. "Return to the ship and we'll see if we can find an empty one."

First, they would traverse the tunnel, fill the cylinders provided by NASA and then enter the lab for the sake of the new members of the crew. They reached the end of the containers and landed the ships. Two members from each ship exited the airlock and proceeded to fill the provided cylinders from the gas port established on the previous mission. When finished, they were processed back into the ships.

"Okay," Marvin said, "let's see if we can locate an empty container." Marvin lead the way as the ships proceeded to the lab complex. At the point where the hallway enlarged in size, Marvin paused. "We haven't checked the floor level in this part of the complex. It's likely that the empties would be stored near where they are using them. Let's go turn on the lights and then return here."

Frank followed close enough to keep a visual as Marvin headed for the routine chore of turning on the lab's lighting system. Then the twin crafts returned to the first enlargement of the stone tunnel next to the lab and slowly descended toward the lower level. About five hundred feet down, the floor appeared. Then, stacked against the walls of the lower lever were dozens of the containers and duplicates of the cylinder in which Roger Stahls was found, alive and well.

"There they are," Marvin said.

When suited and ready, Marvin and Doug picked one of the gravity cubes and headed for the stack of containers. The first stack was two units high. The crown of the top device was some eight feet above the floor. Marvin reached up and set the gravity cube against the glass wall of the top crate and activated it. He and Doug, one on each end, picked up the container and set it down on the floor. He released the cube. Marvin set it on top of the container then boosted Doug up so he could activate it again. When the cube locked itself to the lid Doug jumped back to the floor. Again, on each end, Marvin and Doug lifted it clear of the lower box then stepped over and set it on the floor. Marvin and Doug examined the mating surfaces then looked at each other.

"Tongue and Groove," Doug said. "They used a tongue and groove fit for a seal. Apparently simply by its own weight."

"What do you think this weighs?" Marvin said.

"NASA said the cylinder Roger was in weighed four-point-six times what the equivalent of Earth glass would weigh. Almost 3,000 pounds."

"Another thing," Marvin said. "We will have to strap the crate closed to move it to make sure it doesn't accidentally come open in transit."

Marvin and Frank proceeded to the lab complex and conducted a 'tour' for the sake of the new pilots on board. They all wanted to see the Moon Buggy; it was from Earth, and then, the five enclosures. When finished, while crossing the high wall back toward the offices, Lucas Wilbur leaned forward and stared downward.

"Colonel, look," he said. "Down at the bottom of the wall; it looks like a hole in the wall or another tunnel."

Marvin studied the floor of the hallway. "Yeah, it does. Frank, follow me down; let's look at the floor level."

The two shuttles slowly descended the half-mile to the lower region of the lab complex. Nearing the floor, a tunnel opening came into view. It was of the same dimensions as the entrance tunnel. Marvin hovered in front of it. Frank eased down beside him. The tunnel grew darker the further they looked into it; the influence of the lab lighting gradually faded.

"Apparently this tunnel leads farther down the complex past the five enclosures. They're above us." Marvin said.

"Based on the distance we traveled from the entrance on the other end all the way to the lab, it seems the lab is about the middle of the 'glass mountain' we saw on the surface. There's more here than just the lab and the sleeping giants," Doug said.

"Shall we go in and have a look?" Dave said.

Daniel looked down the darkening tunnel and then in the rear view monitor at the well-lighted lab complex. "What about lighting in there,"

"Let's go in a short distance," Marvin said. He turned on the ship's lights and the search beam and then swiveled the beam to check the tunnel's stone walls. The walls and ceiling all were smooth rock. "Frank," Marvin continued, "let's fly side-by-side on this one. We have plenty of room. It has the same dimensions as the other two tunnels."

"Agreed," Frank said. The crews prepared to advance into new territory.

"Anybody sees anything at all, sound off," Marvin said. "We're entering new ground here that could be hazardous. Everybody stay alert."

Marvin and Frank looked at each other and eased the sticks forward, lights searching ahead. Stone walls slowly passed by the ships as they ventured deeper and deeper into the tunnel.

"Frank," Melissa Ryan said, "something's up there on the right. I can barely see it sticking out from the wall."

"It looks like a set of stairs," Logan Oliver said.

Frank slowed Shuttlecraft Two, Marvin synchronized Shuttlecraft One's speed.

"It is," Daniel said.

The crews leaned forward and followed the stairs through the upper windshield. They went to an opening at the top of the tunnel. The opening was about fifty feet square.

"There's a set of stairs on this side, too!" Joyce Hayden said. "Look at the size of those stairs, there must be three feet from one step to the next." She and the rest of the crew stared at the ceiling. There was a fifty-by-fifty-foot opening there as well.

"Frank," Marvin said, "let's fly through to the second floor, just enough for a visual. If we cannot see each other, back out and we'll do something different. We don't want to get separated."

Frank nodded. "Okay, proceeding up through the opening."

Marvin matched his ascent speed. Momentarily the two ships disappeared through the access holes. On the upper floor, each was in a fifty-foot wide hallway in total darkness, save the illumination of the ship's lights. Moments later they both reappeared at the ceiling level of the lower tunnel.

"Okay," Marvin said. "It appears that each opening leads to something different with large rooms or something between them. Frank, you go first on your side and I'll follow you in. We can find out what's there, and then check this side."

"Going up," Frank said and proceeded up through the access hole with Marvin following close behind. The two ships entered a fifty-foot wide hallway and began to advance farther into a new area. Up ahead there was a large doorway with an arch-shaped top. Frank turned his ship into the opening and flew into a huge volume of darkness. Marvin entered behind him and then took Shuttlecraft One up to his side. Both of the ships lights combined barely illuminated a wall on the far side of the huge chamber.

"How far away?" Frank said.

"Looks to be about a thousand feet or more," Doug said.

Marvin slowly rotated the ship side-to-side to see what might be in the enormous room. Slowly, their eyes began to pick up the thousands of wires, or tiny cables, each hanging from the ceiling to a bucket or pot on the floor. They seemed to be a couple of feet apart and numbering into the thousands. They studied the layout for a few minutes.

"I know what this is," Dave said. "It's a greenhouse or hothouse, they grew food here. There must be a reason why they would grow it inside. I've got a feeling...Colonel, Marvin, let's check the other side."

The two ships made their way back to the opening, down, then up and into the opposite side of the structure. Along the hallway, every hundred feet or so, there was a room and inside each was huge bed. In almost every one there was a petrified body of one of the giants. In the rooms were hand rails mounted on the walls and doors about twenty feet above the floor. In several of the rooms, there were chairs with a single wheel, shaped like a ball, under its center. All were laying on their sides.

All the bodies appeared to be bedridden, and in the last moments, struggled until the end. Many of the bodies were in contorted shapes with the bedclothes twisted in and around their arms and legs. The shadows created by the ship's lighting and the encroaching blackness gave the scene an eerie ghostly atmosphere.

"When the disaster came," Frank said, "these people sacrificed themselves to save the young; the giants in the other end of the complex."

"They made a costly sacrifice, and it was not for naught," Marvin said, "the young people are now sleeping, waiting for us to wake them up."

"This part of the lab, ah, living area gives me the creeps," Logan said.

"Me, too," Daniel said. "It's the avenue of the dead."

"And a tapestry of supreme sacrifice," Melissa added.

"Marvin, Frank, this is a retirement center, assisted living facility, or senior living area," Doug said. "They grew food for them and probably many others, across the hall."

"It sure looks like it," Dave said. Marvin looked across at Shuttlecraft Two.

"Frank," he said, "let's go back down to the main tunnel and check farther down the hallway."

Frank nodded and both pilots rotated their ships and began to retrace their flight paths and descend down through the open holes at the stairs. On the lower level, they turned toward new ground and proceeded cautiously. The smooth walls of the structure flowed past the ships, the lights probing ahead; the first light that had invaded this space in many thousands of years.

The crews slowly became aware of a faint glow ahead, gradually growing brighter. Then they all saw it; a square opening in the ceiling of the tunnel spanning its entire width of three hundred feet. Cautiously, the two pilots eased their crafts to and then under the open port. It was a three-hundred-foot square opening that went straight up about two miles. At the end of it was open space.

"It's a way out!" Doug exclaimed.

"That's good to know," Marvin said. "It looks clear, let's check it out."

The two ships began rising through the shaft, slowly making their way toward the exit at the top of the complex. As the floors passed by the ships the crews searched the interiors. There were more living quarters, some areas that seem like maintenance shops, others like offices, and some storage areas. Near the top, on the left, an open bay came into view.

"That was probably a hangar bay for their ships; they could fly in from the top of the complex," Marvin said.

"Not surprising that it's empty," Doug said. "No doubt they evacuated all that they could."

"Problem is," Daniel said, "there was no place to go. The disaster was too destructive."

The two ships continued upward toward space. Three floors up there appeared, again on the left, another open bay. This time, it was filled with seats lined up like theater seats on Earth.

The enormous seats faced a huge screen at the end of the open room. The two crews hovered their crafts and studied the scene. There was a center aisle a hundred feet wide. At the back of it, there was a huge machine of some type. It was ten-by-ten feet by twenty-feet long. There was a tube sticking out the front of it pointed at the huge screen.

"A theater!?" Daniel said.

"That, or a classroom with video instruction," Dave offered.

Doug glanced at Marvin. "Think what we could learn about this race from that machine."

"It would fit in a Guppy," Marvin said. "However, there's a giant bay door and it's closed."

The crews studied the fifty-foot door mounted on tracks. It apparently was a simple sliding door. Dave studied the tracks. "A Guppy could pull it open. Just hook a towing cable to it and pull it along the tracks enough to gain access."

"That machine could be a very valuable learning tool for Karen and Jean," Doug said, "It would help a great deal in working with the alien language."

"We will return with one of the Guppy's and take it to Earth," Marvin said. I'll talk to Winston about it. It just may be an important part of the giant's ticket to Earth."

Chapter 15

THE THEATRE

Upon touchdown on Earth, the new pilots, having just experienced their first mission to the Moon, petitioned the Colonel to be a part of the mission to be planned to recover the 'theater machine' now waiting on the Moon. Marvin agreed. The additional experience would be valuable. But first there was business to attend to. The extra Moon Gas must be delivered plus the needed information on the containers.

Marvin had a meeting with Winston Stone to clear the mission and to see if the NASA team had any further requests of the excursion ships to complete mission planning to awaken the first giant. The security team requested additional containers of the Moon Gas to guarantee that they could handle any problem and protect the ship on the faithful mission. Marvin set the launch for the following week.

All the personnel that had been selected and were training on the excursion ships toured Discovery, now nearing completion. There were dozens of technicians throughout the ship working on wiring, switches, panels, readouts, and finishing cosmetic chores. The pilots and crews wanted to see the hangar bays, their maintenance areas, and the safety systems. Discovery would be home; a safe place to be. If things went wrong; if you could get here, you would be safe.

Jake Bullard made final preparations in Guppy 1, readying it for a mission to recover another piece of equipment from the Moon. This would probably be the last small ship mission to the Moon before Discovery launched to revive the giants and bring them to Earth to live. This machine they were about to recover was considered to be a vital step in understanding the people that planet Earth was about to adopt as her own.

The Theatre Mission

With the telemetry program loaded, the crews in place, the ships having been serviced, the three-ship Armada launched, once again, for the Moon. The faithful few witnesses were in attendance to watch the launch but most had begun to consider the excursions to the Moon as routine. The talk on the airways now was the approaching day of the awakening. The day that Discovery would launch for the Moon fully equipped and staffed for the historic moment.

Sports bars, clubs, senior centers, and malls were all preparing for the big day. Big screen TV manufacturers couldn't keep up with the demand. All indicated that after the day of the awakening, the saga of the giants would be ongoing. The 'Giant's Channel' was already selling advertising for its debut. There was talk of combining it with the NASA channel in an attempt to take some of the bore out of NASA programming. Many found that raw science did not hold the average citizen's attention very long. However, put in a character forty feet tall and it would change everything.

The Moon

Marvin did the exit speech and then the arrival speech as per the duty of the Captain. The three ships flew through the complex, as usual, entering the second tunnel, and then ascending the three-hundred-foot square shaft. They arrived at the scene of the coveted machine that, hopefully, was loaded with information on this culture. The three ships hovered and reassessed the possibility to retrieve the piece of equipment and return it to Earth.

"The door is about two inches thick," Jim, Guppy 1, observed. "I can drill a hole in it and attach a towing cable."

"It does look like it would slide along the tracks," Jake said. "I could engage moderate power and see if it will open. All we need is about thirty feet to get in and retrieve the machine."

"Okay, proceed," Marvin said. "Be careful."

Jake positioned Guppy 1 at the closing end of the massive transparent door and hovered. Jim and Carl suited up and entered the cargo hold with a diamond drill and towing cable attachments.

Jim positioned his drilling equipment and began the drilling process. First he affixed a half inch bit and drilled a hole. The drill went through it in minutes. He changed the bit and enlarged the hole to a full one inch. He then inserted the end clamp and activated the lock and attached the towing cable. Carl hooked the other end of the cable to Guppy 1's hard-point. The two men returned to the airlock and were processed back into the cabin. They returned to their seats and buckled up for the towing attempt to open the door.

The Holiday Inn – Aurora, IL

Maggie Bowden, NASA astronaut, pilot of Guppy 2, her crew, and their spouses sat at a round table at the Holiday Inn restaurant enjoying their before-dinner drinks. Her husband, Kenneth, manager of an automobile parts house, toasted

Maggie, the astronaut turned Guppy pilot for her accomplishments on 'making the grade' and being selected to pilot Guppy 2 during the mission to the Moon to awaken the giants. Her crew included Nathan Hobbs, American Airlines navigator turned Guppy 2 navigator; Lynn Rowlands, computer programmer, and Victor Waite, a mechanical engineer.

The close-knit crew had been training diligently to ready themselves for the upcoming mission. Their training was to ready them to assist Guppy 1 in transferring the giants in their containers to Discovery's lab to be awakened. They, the dedicated crew, took pride in standing ready to go at any time.

They had no idea that before this evening of camaraderie was over they would be needed a quarter-million miles away, with the lives of the crew of Guppy 1 hanging in the balance.

The Moon

"Colonel," Jake said. "We are ready to pull the door open."

"Okay," Marvin said. "Frank, let's move the shuttles to a safe distance just as a precaution." Marvin and Frank moved Shuttles One and Two across the vertical shaft a hundred feet and held.

"Proceed," Marvin said.

Jake moved the Guppy along the opening direction of the glass door until the slack was taken up and the towing cable became taut. He paused and examined the door and its mounting again, then began to increase power. Gradually the power percentage began to climb. The door moved a few inches then stopped. Jake paused a moment; his power readout was eight percent. He eased it up to ten.

Suddenly, the door popped out of the upper track and cambered over into the open shaft. The taut towing cable caused the door to swing toward the Guppy. It hit the port side rotor pod, ruptured the outer shell, and damaged the mechanism. The rotor pod seized up and came to a stop. The ship cambered to the left momentarily until the starboard rotor pod sensed the loss of power and adjusted its torque.

The huge pane fell past the Guppy and started down the shaft toward the stone floor a mile below. The towing cable, still attached, pulled the Guppy, now at half power, with it. The whiplash effect swung the ship into the glass wall seventy-five feet down. The ship penetrated the wall, lodging itself half way through it. The transparent door bounced once then started downward again. When it reached the end of the cable, it snapped it and the fifty-by-fifty-foot pane began its journey to the floor far below.

"Jake!" Marvin shouted. "Jake, are you okay!"

"Jake, Carl, Jim, Zeke, anybody!" Doug shouted.

Marvin and Frank eased their ships close to the Guppy trying to get a visual on the crew.

Jake slowly began to regain his senses. The safety harnesses were the only things that kept them from being thrown violently against the forward wall of the spacecraft. He became aware of the voices on the intercom. Jake responded in a weak voice.

"Colonel, I hear you."

"Are you okay!?" Marvin repeated.

"I think so," Jake said. He looked at his crew. Carl and Zeke seemed to be having trouble breathing. Jim seemed to be okay.

"Colonel, it looks like two of my crew may have internal injuries. They seem to have labored breathing. Jim looks okay."

"How about your ship?"

Jake scanned the console. "The port rotor pod is dead. Starboard is still running. The cargo hold is breached. The cabin is still holding pressure.

"What's the readouts on the starboard rotor pod?"

"All readouts are normal. Apparently it survived the sudden jolt."

"Good," Marvin said. "It will give you power for heating and cooling."

"Colonel," Jake said. "Go call Maggie and Guppy 2."

"Will do," Marvin said. "Frank, I'm going to fly to the staging area and radio Earth."

"Go ahead, Colonel," Frank said. "We'll stand by here."

The Holiday Inn

Maggie and crew had just finished their meal and were about to order after-dinner drinks. Two NASA personnel inquired at the front desk and were directed to the party's table. Maggie looked up as the couriers approached.

"Mrs. Bowden, there's been an accident on the Moon." Maggie got to her feet and glanced at her crew. They stood and moved to her elbow.

"What happened?"

"They were trying to gain access to a machine by opening a door. The door fell over on the Guppy and destroyed one of the rotor pods. The Guppy crashed into a wall and is now lodged in it. The crew is trapped inside."

"Are they okay?" Maggie said.

"Jake says that two of them are having a little trouble breathing. They impacted the wall pretty hard. The Shuttles don't have enough power to pull the ship out of the wall and free the crew."

"We do," Maggie said glancing at her crew. "Let's get to Earth Base." The Guppy crew looked at their spouses. They all chimed in unison: "Go."

"We have loaded your ship with everything you need when you get there."

Emergency Departure

Maggie flipped the two switches to start the rotor pods of Guppy 2 and then activated the radio.

"Colonel, this is Guppy 2, come in."

"*Maggie*," Marvin said, "*it's good to hear your voice.*"

"Colonel, we launch in twenty-eight minutes. How's the crew doing?"

"They're okay for now. The problem is they are lodged in a glass wall. The shaft is three hundred feet square and the floor is over a mile below them. When the Guppy hit the wall and lodged, the glass door bounced and then snapped the cable and fell all the way to the floor. It's probably going to take considerable force to pull them free. The result will probably be violent swinging and oscillation, when the ship comes free of the wall.

"Understood," Maggie said. "We'll work on a solution."

In route to the Moon Maggie and crew began experimenting with two of the marine lanterns. They simulated the two Guppies. They tied them together with a shoe string and began practicing de-energizing a swinging motion of one hanging under the other. Victor would hold one of the lanterns. Maggie would pull it free of his fingers and observe the swinging motion and attempt to counter it. After an hour of simulation, they discovered the swing could be lessened by 'following' the load downward on its natural path, slowly bringing it to a stop, and then repeating the process. According to the Colonel, there was plenty of room below the ship.

"Hang in there, Jake," Maggie whispered. "We're on our way."

Maggie and crew spotted Shuttlecraft One at the staging area in the central crater. As they approached, it lifted off and headed for the complex. Maggie followed. Shuttle One flew above the complex to the other end, then dropped into an open shaft and began a descent. Maggie entered the shaft and followed. Soon, Marvin slowed and moved the Shuttle to one side to allow Maggie to address the damaged ship. She eased the Guppy down even with Jake's ship and looked at him through the windshield.

"Maggie," Jake said, "it's good to see you."

"Hello, Jake, glad to be here. Do you have insurance?" Maggie grinned.

"Yeah," Jake responded, "you." This time, Jake grinned.

Lynn and Victor suited up and entered the airlock. Nathan removed the atmosphere and opened the ramp and upper door. Maggie eased the ship into line with Guppy 1 and closed on the hard point hitch. Victor attached the towing cable. Lynn attached the opposite end to one of Guppy 2's lead lines that were attached to the ship's center of mass. The two crewmembers re-entered Guppy 2 and buckled in for the operation.

"Okay," Maggie said, "we're ready to pull the ship free. I'm going to have to follow you downward in the shaft. How much depends on how violent the oscillation is. Jake and crew, are you ready?"

"Yes, we're ready here."

"Okay," Maggie said, "engaging power." Maggie gently engaged power, gradually increasing it and carefully monitoring Jake's ship. It slipped a few inches and stopped. The towing cable was completely rigid. Maggie slowly increased the power percentage, the twin rotor pods humming in unison. When she reached sixty percent, suddenly the ship popped out of the hole in the glass wall, creating slack in the towing cable. Guppy 1 arched downward; Maggie followed it down the shaft a hundred feet, slowly bringing it to a stop. The ship swung the other way; Maggie repeated the process. On the fourth swing, the oscillation was virtually gone.

Maggie slowly lifted the damaged ship up, with Shuttle One leading the way, and out of the shaft. Frank followed behind in Shuttle Two. The ships made their way back to the staging area. With Frank calling out distance Maggie set the damaged Guppy 1 on the surface of the central crater and then landed her ship by Jakes. Jake looked across at Maggie through the windshield.

"Maggie, will you marry me." Laughter erupted in all four ships.

Frank aligned Shuttlecraft Two with Guppy 1 and established a link-up. Jake shut down the starboard rotor pod for the final time, patted the outer shell: "Well done my friend," he muttered and then crawled through the connecting tunnel to the safety of Shuttlecraft Two.

Maggie positioned her ship directly above the damaged Guppy 1 and held while two excursion teams secured the ship to Guppy 2. Maggie would tow her home. In route, Frank made arrangements to deliver the ship to the Chicago location to be thoroughly examined and to arrange a replacement.

Since Discovery was nearly ready, the plans to obtain the 'theater' machine were postponed and would be accomplished on Discovery's maiden voyage. It could easily be stored in the mother ship's cargo hold. The access door to the theater machine had been opened at great expense.

Chapter 16

DISCOVERY

The last of the sweeping trucks drove off the twenty-three-acre launching and landing pad of Discovery, the Armada's flagship. The thousand-foot by thousand-foot, four-foot thick concrete foundation would be the home base of mankind's first step to the stars; via Discovery and her support ships. The flagship was flanked by six excursion ships; shuttles, and two guppies; powerful freight haulers designed for ship-to-shore and shore-to-ship transfers of goods, supplies, and crew.

Discovery's mirror finish reflected multiple images of the activity happening around her as she sat majestically in the center of the launch pad. Six shuttles sat evenly spaced around the perimeter and two guppies, one on each side of the enormous entrance ramp, waited for a summons to enter the second deck hanger bay and dock. First destination: The Bonneville Salt Flats and a demonstration for the public that had waited patiently for two years for Discovery's debut.

Half-a-million people would be in attendance at Bonneville to see the interplanetary spaceship fly for the first time. They would put their hopes and dreams aboard for the first voyage to Earth's closest celestial neighbor. The sheer volume of people would be a concern for the National Guard who, in proper precaution, arranged facilities, water trucks, medics, and ample security. Discovery would arrive between one and two p.m.

Thirty Rotor Pods, all humming the same song, now quieted by strategically placed sound dampening partitions, were holding their power in repose waiting for instructions from the bridge.

Forty-two, now highly trained 'Saucernauts,' in orientation since five a.m. and scheduled to man the ships at eight, received their various instructions. Then, six of them, the bridge crew, entered the mother ship, Discovery, and manned the bridge. Then, the significant contributors to the lunar saga, invited to share Discovery's debut, boarded Discovery to share the maiden flight and public demonstration.

Already on board were the maintenance crews assigned to each excursion vessel. They were stationed and housed in the hangar bays. Discovery's Maintenance and Operations Team of eighteen were stationed throughout the ship; eight on the main deck, six on the hanger deck, and four on the upper deck.

Marvin activated the ship-to-ship and initiated the sequence of docking the shuttles and guppies.	The ships all acknowledged and Shuttlecraft One rose off the launch pad, flew to the dead center of the giant windshield of Discovery and then rose to the second deck. The hanger door opened quickly, slowing as it reached the top of its tracks. The shuttle disappeared inside and the door closed. The scene was repeated five more times. Then the guppies both rose to dead center of the rearmost hangar door, wider to accommodate two elongated ships side-by-side. They entered and the door closed and sealed.

As the crews disembarked their shuttles and came down to the main floor of Discovery, some taking the four elevators and some taking the stairs, Marvin looked around at the newly commissioned Discovery.

The volume seemed overwhelming. Discovery was six-hundred feet in diameter and two-hundred feet high in the center. It looked the same from the top and from the bottom. The hull was sectioned into five levels.

The lowermost deck, twenty-feet high, housed the rotor pods and banks of batteries, sectioned to individually support each rotor pod, plus air circulation ducts with dedicated pumps.

The space also housed the nine-legged landing gear; three sets of tripod-type gears to support the enormous weight of the behemoth. The first tripod was positioned at fifty feet from center, the second at one-hundred feet and the third at one-hundred-fifty feet from center to distribute the weight proportionately.

Each of the thirty rotor pods was a separate stand-alone unit, tied together only by electronic connections to work together to drive the enormous ship. A failure, should there be one, would not affect the rotor pods around it. They would automatically 'take up the slack.'

The second level was the main deck. The third level was the second deck dedicated to the housing of the shuttles and guppies and their support teams and supplies.

The fourth level was for the air supply, oxygen, food, water, medical supplies, various tools, and general needs of the two-hundred-eight members of the ship's company.

Level five, the last fifty feet of the ship, was the cargo hold; a volume dedicated to storage of 'finds' and artifacts, to be returned to Earth. The uppermost level could be opened to space without endangering the ship's personnel or it could be pressurized; a feature soon to be praised.

Dead center in the ship, standing on the main deck, one could look straight up and see the sky, or stars. The fifty-foot circular tube went from the main deck to the transparent ceiling. You could see the quarter-moon guard rails fencing off the floors above. On four sides were the structural supports that went all the way to the 'skylight.' Mounted in those walls were the vents for circulation of heating and cooling airflow.

The top of the ship was finished with transparent lead-filled acrylic, a fifty-foot diameter pane of very tough temperature-tolerant material that had proven itself on the NASA space shuttles for years. Such was the material used on the windshield as well.

At Discovery's perimeter, the thickness of the vessel was fifty feet. The three windshield panes were fifty-by-fifty, three across, with another three on the upper side of the ship, and three additional on the lower side of the windshield. A transparent viewing advantage of a hundred and fifty by a hundred and fifty feet.

Video equipment was installed on each side of the windshield, facing ahead. Each excursion craft was equipped the same and channeled to the mother ship to a bank of monitors viewed by safety personnel. These images could be transmitted to Earth as well.

The close quarters of the original Research One had set the precedent on spaceships. And it afforded just slightly more room inside than the space shuttles, which were a little more than the Apollo ships, which again were not a lot more than the earlier capsules that gallantly flew in years gone by. But now, inside the spaceship in which

Marvin was standing, Shuttlecraft One could easily fly around inside the main deck.

The bridge was a raised floor a foot and a half above the sprawling main deck. It was a hundred and fifty feet wide, fifty feet from the windshield, and contoured with its symmetry. The same was cordoned off by a waist-high banister.

The main deck housed all the crew's quarters, a conference room, a galley and cafeteria, three lounges centered on the portholes, a linguistics lab, a research lab, a hospital, a clinic, and a brig.

Located behind the rearmost hangar bay, the home of the guppies, on the second deck, was the facility to accommodate the waking of the giants. The chamber was one-hundred by one-hundred by fifty-feet high, with two airlocks located at the back of the hangar bay and lab.

The room, for security reasons, could be sealed from the rest of the ship by activating a built-in system. It had its own air supply and heating and cooling system. Further, it was equipped with a system that would release a concentrate of the 'Moon Gas,' should the waking giant become dangerous and threaten the integrity of Discovery. It was known as Karen and Jean's Interview Room. The first giant scheduled was the first in the row of glass crates, affectionately known as 'Big John.' A transfer canister had been fashioned so the supply line to his suspended animation unit could be cut, the canister attached to continue his supply and pressure, and then be transferred to Discovery. Then the interview.

Chapter 17

THE DEDICATION

Marvin, Frank, Doug, and Dave scanned the console of Discovery. All indicators were green and ready for flight. Frank's eyes went to the new display, a round wireframe schematic of Discovery, twenty-four inches in diameter. On it were dot's, representing the thirty rotor pods and where they were located in Discovery's frame. All thirty lights were green.

Marvin gently eased the left-hand stick rearward. The giant version of the original Research One, now the flagship of the Armada, slowly lifted its nine landing struts clear of the pad on which it had spent two years taking shape.

The usual hum of the rotor pods was effectively canceled out by the dampening plates. The greatly increased mass of the ship resulted in a gentle initiation of movement. There was something special about it. The awesome power, breaking the bonds of Earth, could be felt.

When the sensors registered twenty feet from the launch pad, all nine landing struts retracted in unison and disappeared into the bottom of the ship, closing the ports and making the bottom of the ship smooth and aerodynamic. Marvin raised the ship to five-hundred feet, turned west and pushed the right-hand stick forward. Discovery responded smoothly; the onboard computers reading millions of lines of code. Marvin entered **500** on the speed. Bonneville Salt Flats and half-a-million people were three hours away.

"Twenty miles," Marvin said. "Disengaging Auto-Flight; going on manual. All crews to your shuttles."

Very quickly the half-Moon sea of people came into view; a huge marker of Discovery's destination. An enormous 'X' had been laid out on the Salt Flat to mark the spot to land Discovery adjacent to some vehicles. A platform with an announcer and a system of speakers had been placed so everyone could hear.

The president and his entourage and the NASA administrator and his staff were in attendance. They both had 'entertained' the masses with dedications and praises for the forthcoming display of a unified effort of their government. They were enjoying the rare praise of the people for the handling of their money.

Marvin moved Discovery into position and hovered over the 'X' at five-hundred feet and held for several minutes to allow the viewing public time to enjoy the moment and give the crews time to ready their various crafts for the demonstration.

He then began a slow descent. From the ground's perspective, the giant ship slowly got larger and larger. Marvin stopped the descent at on-hundred feet for the viewing advantage of the onlookers and manually activated the lowering of the landing gear. Nine spider legs erupted from the bottom of the gleaming craft.

Holding at one-hundred feet the shuttles began emerging from Discovery one at a time and stationing themselves on each side of the ship. The reaction of fascination with the scene could be heard from the viewers. The shuttles hovered, three on each side of Discovery. Then the guppies emerged from behind the ship and made their way on either side of the lineup.

The guppies produced a greater reaction in the viewing public as they noted the unusual shape of the freight-dedicated craft. They looked very similar to the old steamships that sailed the Mississippi; the ones that had the paddlewheels mid-ship on each side. Except, on the guppies, the 'paddle wheels' were spherical, housing a rotor pod each. They were twenty-four feet wide with the cargo hold twelve feet wide, fifty feet long, and twelve feet high.

Marvin then ordered the Armada to land. In unison, the nine ships slowly descended and touched down. All the ramps opened and the crews came out to wave at the crowd and listen to the announcer inform the crowd of their duties and forthcoming mission to the Moon. The speechmaking lasted twenty minutes; the last five minutes to a 'getting restless' crowd. Now, what they came to see.

Discovery rose off the Salt Flats, turned toward the north and held. The shuttles rose one at a time and assumed a 'point' of a six-pointed star around the flagship. Shuttles One through Six formed the star pattern, then the two guppies positioned themselves behind the formation.

Marvin, remaining at one-hundred feet, talked the formation through three choreographed flyovers of the viewers at a very slow ten miles per hour. The third trip around Marvin steered Discovery back to the center of the demonstration area. The shuttles and guppies positioned themselves around the mother ship and held. Then Marvin ordered the last choreographed part of the demonstration.

The excursion crafts began the ritual of returning to Discovery in reverse order. The two guppies were first and then Shuttles Six down to Two. Then Shuttlecraft One, originally 'Research One' and Discovery sat suspended in the air, side by side, before the public. Discovery slowly initiated a rotation in place to the left until she was facing Research One. Then she eased up close, leaving a twenty-foot clearance. Research One then slowly rotated toward the mother ship. The two ships faced each other, twenty feet apart, one, twenty-four feet in diameter, the other, six-hundred feet in diameter.

As the ships held in place, President Howell made the announcement: "Research One, today, officially hands the Scepter to Discovery. Research One is now and forever Shuttlecraft One."

Shuttlecraft One, accompanied by a tremendous din of cheering and applause, slowly rose up to the hangar deck of Discovery and entered her hangar bay and the door closed. There was applause for several minutes sweeping through a half-million attendees.

Chapter 18

LAUNCH

Discovery sat on its launching pad at Earth Base with its massive entrance ramp full open prior to a 10:30 a.m. launch to the Moon and into history. Barricades surrounding the ship were enforced by the National Guard. The crowd to witness history were enthusiastically cheering and enjoying the moment.

Marvin and his bridge crew were standing on the entrance ramp, inside the spacious airlock, discussing the mission and waving at the crowd sporadically. The shuttles and guppies were in their bays moored securely. The ship's compliment of 208 was on board and making final arrangements for launch in just over two hours.

A disturbance began at the barricade just outside the ramp. Marvin stepped over and looked toward the group of guardsmen. An older man, with a cane, had ducked under the cordoning tape and was making his way toward the ramp. The guardsmen had stopped him and were gently trying to escort him back to the barrier.

"But you don't understand," the senior exclaimed, "I'm not going to live long enough the wait. I have to go now."

"Sir, you can't board the ship," a guardsman explained, "only the crew that's going to the Moon can board the ship."

The man leaned toward Discover's ramp. "I don't have very much time left; I have to go now," the man cried out.

Marvin walked down the ramp. "Let him through," he instructed the guard.

The team of guardsmen looked at Marvin. "Sir, we..."

"It's okay, let him through," Marvin said firmly.

The guardsmen released the older man and steadied him on his feet. "Yes, Sir," they responded and returned to their post.

Marvin extended his arm and hand and nodded toward the ramp. "Come with me."

The older man looked at Marvin. "I have to go with you right now," he said again. The gentleman walked to the ramp and started up it, pausing to check his balance on the incline. Marvin took his arm and steadied him. Together they went up the ramp, through the airlock, and made their way across the eighty-foot span of metal floor to the raised bridge area. Marvin assisted him up the two steps to the bridge floor then to the Captain's chair. The senior looked up at Marvin, smiling. Marvin indicated the chair. The man stepped to a position in front of it then sat down holding his cane in front of him. A smile spread across his face, then his eyes went to the massive windshield and the view outside. People, many of them children, were waving at the crewmembers of the ship. The man waved back, smiling. He looked again at Marvin, then at the console with its multiple displays and readouts, then back to Marvin's face.

The senior took a labored breath. "When do we leave?"

"In about two hours," Marvin said noticing his stress. "Are you okay?"

The senior studied Marvin's face for a long moment then looked around and the main deck and the sea of young faces about to embark on the adventure of a lifetime. Each of them was full of energy and motivation. His eyes found Marvin's face again. He got to his feet with some difficulty. "You better do this," he said. "I'm not in too good a shape. I had a stroke."

Marvin nodded then pointed at the monitoring cameras mounted on each side of the windshield. "See that TV camera? Everything I see through this windshield you will see on your TV at home. Each one of the small ships is now equipped with monitoring cameras that will also show on your TV at home. We will see it at the same time. We are going to take this adventure together.

The man looked at the floor and then back at Marvin. "My TV ain't no good; it won't come on."

Marvin took the man's arm. "Come with me," he said. He walked him back down the ramp and motioned to the news team. An announcer hurried over to talk to Marvin.

"I want a big screen TV in this man's home by launch," Marvin said. "Charge it to me."

The senior perked up and patted Marvin on the shoulder and looked at the announcer. The announcer's eyes lit up. "We won't have to Colonel. Any TV sales outlet will jump on this." The announcer escorted the older man toward the building talking rapidly and taking notes. Marvin returned to his ship.

"Nice, Colonel," Frank said, "very nice."

"Everybody has hopes and dreams,' Marvin said.

"I'm one of them," Frank said.

Into History

Discovery, her eight shuttles, two-hundred-eight souls, and the curiosity and need-to-know of millions left the launch pad and majestically rose above Aurora. The city quickly dropped away as the thirty rotor pods labored in unison.

Marvin activated the intercom. "All personnel, this is the Captain; my famous speech. Check your safety harnesses for proper adjustment. We are passing through the satellite belts and debris field of the earth. We could get some strong lateral movement from the AVS system." A sea of hands pulled on belts and straps, some of the 'first timers' overdoing it, only to readjust them again a few minutes later.

Soon, the first 'intersection' was reached and the six-hundred-foot disc cambered to the left a few degrees, then assumed a straight line of flight. Discovery had found a clear path to true outer space. The belts came off and the ship's company began to relax and enjoy the ride. The atmosphere was abuzz with plans and suggestions. Groups of similar interest began to form, some making their way to one of the ship's three lounges.

Astronauts Maggie Bowden and Jake Bullard, pilots of Guppies One and Two, and their respective crews sat around a table in the aft lounge. They were discussing the intricacies of handling the glass crates while transporting the giants to Discovery. The crates were just under six feet wide, according to Daniel's cloth tape, and just under four feet high and, likewise, just under fifty feet long. The crew wondered if that was an indication that the giant's system of measure was metric. It was noted by discussion that when everything was established for the mass-moving of hundreds of them, two of the crates at a time would fit in the guppy's cargo hold. They could transport two giants each to Discovery, pick up two empty crates, and return them to the tunnel. The one concern in the operation would be the time element. They had only a minute to detach the crate, attach the portable pressure system, and seal off the severed pipe in the floor of the tunnel. Any longer and the giant could awaken on the way to Discovery, creating a possible disaster. They mutually agreed that they were ready for the task.

Marvin signaled the five maintenance supervisors, called them aside and suggested they pick a couple of each of their teams and circulate about the ship with an eye for anything loose that might be a problem during the mid-point free-floating turn around and reversal of power. The team of engineers that designed Discovery had pointed out that the most difficult task involved in the construction of Discovery was arranging the substructure so that, when weightlessness was present, nothing floated away.

The twenty-four seats lined across the windshield, twelve on each side of the six-seat bridge operations center, were occupied with different faces. The awesome view afforded by the massive 'window' was mesmerizing. Also, the three thirty-foot diameter portholes, starboard, port, and aft had dedicated viewers stationed at each. Each also was a location of one of the ship's three lounges.

Two hours into the mission, Marvin again keyed the ship's intercom.

"All crewmembers, mid-point turnaround for the deceleration part of the transit Earth-to-Moon is coming up soon. I'm sure all of you remember from the classroom that the weightless period during Discovery's turnaround is four minutes because of the much greater mass of the vessel. This is to make the angular torque at the perimeter of the vessel within safety limits. Remember that there are barf bags behind each seat. If you need to use them, do so. Let's keep this, our home for the next several days, clean."

As the miles rolled by, the ship's company took turns at the windshield, looking downward watching the Earth grow smaller and smaller and the Moon in the upper windshield get larger. In the immense volume of space, Discovery and Research One may as well have been the same size. Only its occupants could appreciate the difference. It was a matter of scale.

'Twenty minutes until Zero-G transfer to deceleration phase,' came from the voice mode of the telemetry computer.

The crew headed for their seats and the securing straps. Marvin glanced at the maintenance team. They nodded readiness. Some of the crew were hurrying down the stairs from the upper decks and taking their seats and buckling up. Several of them pulled out the barf bag and placed it under a strap handy to be reached.

"They have been to one of the lounges and apparently found the cuisine appealing," Marvin said. Doug nodded, smiling.

When the last warning timed out, the telemetry program cut power. The huge ship, with a nudge, began a four-minute rotation around the horizontal axis. The crewmembers displayed many different visible reactions to the sensation. Some appeared unaffected; others seemed to be trying to hold their breath until it was over. Several deployed the barf bags and threatened but managed to contain. A few got the job done.

'Thirty seconds until 1-G deceleration phase.'

Marvin watched the crew as the ship powered up and began decelerating to stop at the Moon. They very quickly adjusted back to the world of weight supplied by a changing velocity.

Chapter 19

BIG JOHN

Discovery touched down on the Moon. The pilots of the Armada agreed on a methodology of 'flying at ground level.' Due to the enormous weight of Discovery, upon landing the pilot would set the *surface* as the altitude of the spacecraft. Therefore, if the surface collapsed under the ship, it would remain flying at ground level following a brief reaction. The excursion ships would practice the same precaution.

"All personnel," Marvin began, "stay alert, take no chances, report anything out of the ordinary. Let everybody go back home together, perhaps with a couple of friends." He paused for a moment then began laying out the procedure to take care of the first order of business; waking Big John.

"All excursion crafts work in pairs; no ships out alone. Joyce Hayden, Shuttlecraft Three and Tim Woodward, Shuttle Four take your crews and fly to the crater and tunnel entrance and scout for a smooth place to land Discovery. Melissa Ryan, Shuttlecraft Five and Logan Oliver, Shuttlecraft Six you and your crews go to the piling and get four of the gravity cubes in each craft and bring them back here to Discovery. We will need them to handle the glass crates. Jake Bullard, Maggie Bowden, and crews, prep the guppies for retrieval of Big John.

"Let's get these things done and Discovery spotted close to the tunnel. By then it will be late evening on Earth. We can have a meal, go over everything with Earth Base and then get some rest. Tomorrow morning, we can proceed with the task."

The respective crews energetically went about their assignments. Shuttlecraft Three and Shuttlecraft Four launched and headed for the crater hole in the glass mountain. They flew up to the rim of the crater and began circumnavigating it, from a height of a hundred feet, at first, looking for an area relatively smooth and level at least six-hundred feet wide and long.

Two possibilities presented themselves; one in line with the complex and the other between the complex and the central crater. They first combed the in-line prospect, flying at ground level. Several holes and cracks were observed. Next, they checked the area to the side, toward the central crater. Flying next to the ground they were satisfied with the stability of the surface and reported back to the mother ship.

Marvin assumed the pilot's chair to move Discovery. He then activated the radio.

"Shuttlecraft Five, this is Marvin."

"Roger, Colonel, we have the eight cubes. We will arrive at Discovery in about two minutes."

"Roger, we'll wait until you dock. We are ready to move Discovery near to the tunnel opening."

"Roger, approaching Discovery." Marvin watched the indicator lights on the console that confirmed the docking of the shuttlecrafts. They were yellow, waiting for the moorings to secure the ships, the dock doors to close, and the system to pressurize the shuttle bay. Moments later, they were all green.

Marvin activated the intercom. "All personnel. We are moving Discovery to the selected site." Discovery rose from the lunar surface and began the transit of the central crater. Shortly, Marvin saw the two shuttles hovering about a thousand feet apart. The area between them looked smooth and clear of boulders and craters. They were hovering on either side of the site, facing it. Marvin carefully eased Discovery down to the surface and hovered at fifty feet. He rotated the behemoth slowly until the Bridge was facing the opening to the tunnel and touched down on the surface.

Night fell, by the clock, on the city of 'Discovery, Moon,' population 208. The first *evening was spent with video contact with Mother Earth with interviews with many of the personnel on board regarding their expertise and goals on the Moon.*

A walking tour was given of Discovery via remote camera and many impromptu meetings and brief discussions ensued. All were asked their feelings on the event scheduled for the next morning. All were looking forward to it; all hoped it went well. All three lounges were places of much discussion.

The event to follow when Earth awakened in the morning was the subject of much discussion and some predictions. All wondered how the giants would feel when they awakened and found everybody else, except them, was about a foot tall, comparatively. They weren't giants, until us. While they slept and the millenniums passed the only living planet, Earth, was scaled to our size.

The Next Day

"All personnel," Marvin began, "the news people on board Discovery will begin live broadcasting momentarily. Launch all six shuttles; Shuttles One and Two in the tunnel, Shuttles Three and Four just outside the tunnel in the crater, and Shuttles Five and Six just outside Discovery. Guppy

1 will go and get the 'star of the show' when everyone is in position."

Jake Bullard, the pilot of Guppy 1, and his three-man crew were ready. Jim Blalock was his 'saw man,' selected from the fabrication crew who assembled Discovery. Dennis Waters was the 'gas man,' also from the construction team. He had plumbed the hundreds of air tanks, valves, and pressure gauges incorporated into Discovery's design. The fourth, Zeke Springer, was a floater that effectively worked half the skilled jobs during Discovery's creation, filling if for breaks, no shows, and quitters.

Jim had practiced with his diamond saw on many of the pieces of the mysterious material brought back to Earth on previous missions. He knew he had to get the pipe connecting the container to its supply cut very quickly so Dennis could restore Big John's gas supply and pressure before the residual in the container ran out. The powerful saw, designed by NASA, had begun to feel like an extension of his hand and arm. Jim was confident that he could save his 'brand new forty-foot-tall' friend.

Dennis, handler of the gas supply and pressure assembly, had used a duplicate 'dummy' and practiced attaching his equipment after Jim's practice cuts, each session improving his time. His *record was eleven seconds, his average sixteen seconds. He was ready.*

The news team watched Guppy 1 exit its hangar bay on its way to the stone tunnel and Big John's suspended animation unit. Shuttlecraft Two, positioned far enough into the tunnel to allow space for the freight hauling guppy to enter, stood by to assist the retrieval team should they need it.

Upon notice that Guppy 1 had launched, three of Shuttle Two's crew, suited and ready, were processed outside. The guppy circumnavigated Discovery and then became visible on the main cameras on the bridge.

The news announcer was then featured momentarily on the screen. He briefly reminded the audience of millions that it was possible for the episode of waking Big John to go very badly, though not likely, and they should inform all viewing with them.

Further, there were doctors standing by in the lab where the giant would be awakened to do what they could to help, should Big John be in distress when awakened. The announcer pointed out that none of the doctors had ever had a patient with a heart the size of a microwave oven. The screen switched back to the telecast of Guppy 1 about to enter the tunnel. The video feed was switched to Shuttlecraft One now hovering inside the tunnel, opening with its camera on Big John's glass crate. When Guppy 1 dropped down into the crater and approached the tunnel opening, Jackson During, piloting Shuttlecraft One, rotated the ship to follow the Guppy with the camera.

The large personnel and freight transporter moved into the center aisle, aligned itself with Big John's container and touched down. The end ramp of the machine slowly lowered and bumped on the stone floor. Then the door raised to full open. Three of the four-man crew, suited and already in the vacuum of the cargo hold, approached the unit carrying the tools to detach it and bring it aboard.

Jim studied the incoming two-inch pipe momentarily, laid his gloved hand in it and pulled. Satisfied that it was solidly mounted he readied his saw and then looked toward the guppy. "Captain," he said, "ready to cut."

"Stand by," Jake responded, and then radioed Discovery. "Colonel, we are ready to cut Big John loose and bring him aboard."

"Roger that," Marvin responded and took a breath, "proceed and good luck."

"Yes, Sir," Jake said, nodding to Jim.

Jim noted the three crewmembers from Shuttle Two standing by and the position of the gas supply, and then activated the powerful saw. He engaged the pipe and exerted pressure. He felt the resultant vibration from the tool as the blade began to sink into the pipe. Twenty seconds later the blade exited the other side. He quickly rolled out of the way giving access to Dennis. Dennis placed the assembly at the end of the pipe and locked the flex tube onto the open end leading to Big John's container to stop the gas loss. Then he grabbed the dead-end assembly and placed it over the incoming severed pipe, locked the choke valve, stopped the flow, and read the gauge: twelve-point-two pounds per square inch. He quickly dialed the same on the pressure assembly and set it on top of the container.

"Okay, the container is secure," he said, "let's get the straps on it." They quickly, with help from the three crewmen from Shuttle Two, affixed the two straps around the unit. Then, using the gravity cubes, they moved Big John into Guppy 1 for transport to Discovery.

The three suited members of Guppy 1 stayed in the cargo hold with their passenger. The TV cameras caught the departure of Guppy 1 from the tunnel into the crater.

The viewing link was changed to Discovery once again and showed Guppy 1 emerge from the crater and head for Discovery. When the ship passed out of view of Discovery's main cameras the news crew cleverly switch to the camera covering the hangar bay and the 'interview room.'

Access had been cleared; hangar bay door open, airlock to the lab open, and cameras rolling. Guppy 1 entered the bay, dispatched Big John by the hands of the suited members, and moved him all the way into the lab, unstrapped the container's lid and then exited. The airlock was closed and the lab pressurized. The interpreting machine, programmed by the Linguistics Institute, mounted in a cabinet and on rollers, was placed in the lab near the wall by the adjacent offices. It was there to change Big John's utterances into English and the linguistics team's into Big John's tongue.

Earth

"This has got to go well," President Walter Howell said staring at the TV monitor. He looked around at Winston Stone and NASA's supervisory entourage.

"It will," Winston Stone said. "It's on TV." The president took a nervous breath; the snippet didn't help.

Once again, Grand Central Station was a sea of curious faces watching the monitors as the moment approached that the world would make its first contact with someone 'not from here.' Once again ninety percent of the world's TV's would be tuned in.

Discovery – The Moon

Professor Charles Liggins, Anthropologist, and his entourage, with Karen and Jean, entered the lab through the adjacent offices. The security team, with the sleeping gas at the ready, was standing by. A team of four entered the pressurized lab and shut off the gas supply affixed to the unit. They removed the lid from the container and laid it aside, and then exited the room. All eyes in Discovery and millions watching electronically were on Big John.

Planet Earth waited in silence for just over a minute. Then Big John opened his eyes, blinked several times, and scanned the ceiling. He reached up with his hand as if to touch the lid of the container. Discovering it was gone he sat up. He paused a moment, rubbed his eyes and looked around. He saw the lid of the unit lying on the floor beside the device. He blinked several times, got out of the container and began to examine the room. He began walking around the room pushing on the walls, and then reached up and pushed on the ceiling, gradually becoming more and more agitated.

"He's confused and probably scared," Professor Liggins said. "Karen, Jean, step out where he can see you; he's seen you before, maybe he'll remember. Stay close to the door." Karen and Jean nodded, stepped out into the lab a few steps and waved their arms. Nothing, no response.

"Hey," Karen said in a raised voice. Still no response. Jean stepped out a little farther, cupped he hands around her mouth and shouted.

"Hellooooo!"

A hush fell on planet Earth and swept throughout the ship.

Apparently, Big John did not hear or did not believe the sound was really there.

"Hello, I'm talking to you!" Jean shouted again. Still no reaction. The giant was pushing on the ceiling again. Jean paused a moment and then reached down and pulled off her right shoe and threw it at Big John. It hit him on the nose. He stopped dead in his tracks, looked down, and saw the tiny shoe land on the floor. He reached down and picked it up between his thumb and forefinger and examined it. Jean and Karen waved their arms again.

"Hello...over here," Jean repeated in a raised voice. This time, Big John looked over at the wall of the lab and spotted Karen and Jean. He was frozen in place for a long moment. Jean smiled. Big John returned the smile, crossed his legs, and sat down on the lab floor. Still holding Jean's shoe, he stared at Karen and Jean, both the equivalent of about one foot tall. Jean took a few steps closer to Big John. His eyes followed her.

"Careful," Karen whispered.

Jean looked around briefly and nodded. She looked up a Big John and extended her hand, palm up. Big John looked at her hand, at the shoe, then back at her hand. He reached out and dropped it in her hand. Jean put her shoe back on. Karen stepped up to Jean's side. Big John uttered several words in his language, his voice very low pitched, then waited, watching Karen and Jean. Karen stepped over to the language computer and looked at the screen. There were several words in disjointed sequence. She studied them.

"He acts like a child or maybe a teenager," Charles Liggins said stepping out to be visible to Big John. Big John glanced at the professor momentarily and then his eyes went back to Karen at the interpreting machine.

Karen looked around. "On the screen are the words, 'I...*where...am ... locate.*' Ah, he wants to know where he is." Karen thought for a moment then stepped over and activated the intercom.

"Colonel, he needs to see outside. We need to secure the lab airlock, depressurize the Guppy's hangar bay and open the outer door."

"Do it, gentlemen," Marvin said. "Karen, it looks like you've made contact with a very young citizen. I wonder if they are all about his age?"

"They could be," Professor Liggins responded. "In a desperate and dire situation, they could have made the decision to use what resources they had to save as many of the young people as they could. No doubt they knew it was a big gamble but with no alternative, they simply did it."

Karen typed into the language machine: You are in a spaceship on the Moon. She then pushed the **INTERPRET** key. A line of symbols appeared on the screen. Karen looked up at Big John and pointed at the screen. He leaned forward and stared at it.

The hangar door, visible through the transparent airlock, raised to full open. Big John's eyes went to the hangar door opening eighty feet away and the surface of the Moon in the distance, then back to the screen. He got to his feet, walked over and placed his hands on the airlock and pushed on it.

"No!" Karen said loudly. Big John stopped and looked at her. She quickly typed on the keyboard again: *You can't go out there; your home was destroyed.* She waved her arms and pointed at the screen again. He stepped back and studied it. A few moments later he sat back down on the floor of the lab and put his head in his hands. Karen and Jean looked at each other.

"He didn't know," Jean said. "Apparently they didn't tell them. They must have put them to sleep first then moved them to the suspended animation units."

Professor Liggins motioned to Karen and Jean. "See if you can find out why they were here on the Moon. If he was born here. What this place is."

Big John raised his head up and spoke a short phrase. Karen hurried over to the screen and spent a few moments putting the rudimentary words together. "He wants to know if his parents are still alive." Karen looked up a Big John then approached the keyboard again and typed in: "*Where do they live*?" He looked at the screen for a moment then shook his head.

"He doesn't understand what you mean," Jean said. Karen typed: *Where did they home?* Big John responded with a single word. Karen studied the screen. "The fourth planet—Mars?"

Daniel Stubblefield, glued to the monitor quickly keyed in and spoke: "Karen, to him the fourth planet is the asteroid belt, before the explosion of course. Mercury wasn't in the planet line-up. It was a moon."

"Oh, yeah, it would be," Karen said. "He's from the exploded planet, originally. But, why is he here?"

Karen, Jean, Professor Liggins, and his entourage continued with the audacious task of discovering the status of the sleeping giants, the reason for the lunar Arcology, and what they might know about the state of the rest of the solar system prior to the horrendous disaster that destroyed this magnificent city and research lab. Meanwhile, Marvin and the ship's company began the task of gathering available artifacts to be returned to Earth for study.

Marvin dispatched Shuttlecraft Two and Guppy 1 to go to the underground library where Research One and her original crew had found the books and rings and a teaching machine. They were commissioned to get the remainder of the books and the machine. They had borrowed one of Discovery's most useful tools; one of Jim's diamond saws.

Shuttlecraft Three and Guppy 2 were dispatched to the piling to get the remainder of the gravity cubes. They were to transport them to the cargo hold and secure them. Shuttles Four and Five were dispatched to the lab complex to check for more of the desktop machines and retrieve all. It was believed that there was such a computer for each operation performed in the huge lab, each with a wealth of knowledge for mankind. With the excursion crafts out on their mission and then returning laden with precious treasure to grace the cargo hold, the theater machine came to mind.

Shuttlecrafts One and Two, with Guppy 2, were dispatched to the vertical shaft at the other end of the lab complex to retrieve the theater machine and bring it to the cargo hold of Discovery.

The machine was tethered to Maggie's ship and moved to the cargo hold of the mother ship without incident.

As Marvin watched the cargo doors close over the prize he thought about Winston Stone's 'out of the way' comment after being informed of the accident with Guppy 1 and Maggie's gallant rescue. He'd said to a colleague: "Considering the difficulty of getting that thing here, it better not start showing reruns of *I Love Lucy*."

The team working with Big John gradually, bit-by-bit, learning who he is, why he's here, and where he came from, soon reached a staying point. Big John must be fed and the team must rest and have a meal as well. Professor Liggins suggested vegetable soup for the guest giant. He believed he would surely be a vegetarian in closed city living. The ship's galley prepared Big John two gallons of vegetable soup, a gallon of water, and two loaves of bread. Further, ample bedding with blankets, quilts, and pillows was supplied. Karen typed into the interpreter: *Eat. Sleep. Rest.* Big John stared at the screen for a long moment then turned his gaze to Karen and Jean. His eyes moistened, then he picked up the container of soup, stuck his finger in it and then into his mouth, then again, then drank a third of it in one gulp. He then bit off a half a loaf of bread, chewed three or four times, took a sip of water and swallowed it.

"He's a teenager," Charles Liggins said. In five minutes he finished the food. He looked again at Karen and Jean for a moment, then laid down on the 'guest bed' and closed his eyes. Minutes later the very noticeable deep breathing of sleep filled the lab.

Karen, Jean, Professor Liggins, and their staff notified the security team stationed at the lab that they were headed for the main deck conference room. The bridge crew would meet them there for a preliminary report and some decision making. Marvin radioed the security team.

"He appears to be docile; hopefully, he is, but stay alert. Your first duty is to the ship."

"Yes, Sir," was the response.

The news team positioned their mobile cameras in the main conference room on Discovery's main deck. The video feed was established feeding privately through to NASA's security headquarters. The President, his staff, the NASA director, and his team were standing ready.

Around the conference table on Discovery, Karen, Jean, Professor Liggins, his assistants, and the bridge crew gathered to learn the extent of Karen's and Jean's and the professor's progress so far with the first awakened giant. The White House and NASA had two-way access to the conference.

Karen began: "The language computer we programmed at the Linguistics Institute isn't perfect. However, it is enabling us to communicate with a completely alien language base; a miracle to me. Now, some of the things I am going to relate to you may be altered somewhat in the future as we get better and better able to communicate with these people. What I am going to tell you is, I believe, ninety percent accurate or perhaps better.

"His name is Kronos. I chose the spelling by the sound when he says his name. To get him to say it I pointed at myself and said my name; pointed at Jean and said her name; then the professor. Then I pointed at him. He said Kronos. He's the equivalent of about fourteen to sixteen years old. He was born on the planet that exploded; now the Asteroid Belt. The best name we are able to give his home planet so far is Solaris 4. They designate the planets in the Solar System by naming the star; the Sun; then affixing a number. In his Solar System of thousands of years ago his planet was the fourth planet from the Sun. He and 1,600 others were assigned to work here on the Moon as part of their academic training. I get the impression that they haven't been here very long. According to our count of the giants, four hundred of them didn't make it. He doesn't know that yet.

"He personally worked here in a garden or greenhouse raising food. He said the elders put him to sleep. The next thing he remembers is when he saw me and Jean looking at him through his glass case and then in the lab of Discovery. He's very upset. He doesn't understand the extent of what's happened. We are fortunate that he's mild natured. I get the impression that they are extremely disciplined. We are going to need a long time to work out good communication with him; all of them.

"Colonel, he indicated that six Counselors, sent with him and his class, were also put to sleep. With our rudimentary communications with him, we can't determine exactly what he means. But this we know, there are six giants, three male, and three female, somewhere in the group of 1,200 that are older; more mature. We need to find one of them and wake up him or her." Karen seated herself. There was a moment of silence.

"Mrs. Hastings." President Howell said. "You and Mrs. Henson have done a magnificent job working with this situation. Mrs. Henson, I like your approach."

"He was getting out of control, Mr. President. I didn't want to have to put him back into oblivion. I wanted him to have a chance."

"I'm impressed. I may throw a few shoes the next time I deal with Congress." There was random chuckling around the table.

"Okay," the president continued. "What I understand from your report is that we can bring all these people to Earth to live."

"Yes, Sir. The gravity of their home world was greater than the gravity of Earth."

"Very well. We will begin preparations. We are going to need a small town for 1,200 residents, seven times normal size."

"First thing tomorrow morning, Earth time, we'll dispatch two ships to search the tunnel and find one of the mature giants," Marvin said.

'Night' settled in on the portable city on the Moon. Two hundred and eight residents, and one guest; Kronos: a forty-foot-tall teenager, deep in natural sleep for the first time in thousands of years; having been 'tucked in' by a concerned benefactor one-foot tall. Discovery, with the power plant the equivalent of a town of 1,200, was the

first shelter offered to a people whose 'home' had been ripped away by an ancient disaster. Many of the Earthmen and women on board wrestled with their feelings of a changed world well into the night.

Chapter 20

THE COUNSELOR

Shuttlecrafts One and Two, with Guppy 1, flew in formation to the crater. Then leaving Shuttle Two behind, hovering in the crater at the intersection point of the transmission beam coming from the transponder, Shuttle One and Guppy 1 entered the stone tunnel. The guppy landed just inside the tunnel to wait for a location to pick up one more of the units and deliver it to the examination room aboard Discovery. Shuttle One positioned herself above the containers and began a slow flight, just above them, into the tunnel, searching for an aging face.

The minutes turned into an hour, and then two, as the young faces passed under the watchful eyes of an alert crew. Then, near the half-way point, the spoken alarm was heard.

"Colonel, we've found one. He looks older."

"Guppy 1," Marvin said. "Go. Bring him aboard."

"Aye, Sir," Jake Bullard said and proceeded to fly down the tunnel and secure the container indicated by Shuttle One. Half an hour later they were on their way to the 'interview room' to deliver another challenge to Professor Liggins and the linguistics team.

Aboard Discovery, having been informed that a candidate for an adult giant had been located and was being retrieved and brought aboard, Karen and Jean began the difficult task of communicating the event to Kronos. He would have to be moved into the lab-to-ship airlock to allow the lab to be open to the vacuum of space to bring in the second unit.

Kronos was moved into the airlock and sealed in. The path to space was opened for the incoming container. Ship's personnel, in pressure suits, stationed themselves to receive the device and remove the straps from the sealing lid. Kronos watched the preparations through the transparent walls of the airlock. He was glued to the wall as the crew moved the crate into the lab with the gravity cube on the side of it, then activated its release and left the lab.

Slowly the pressure was brought up to equalization in the lab. Then the crew returned and removed the gas pressure device and the lid of the unit. The tense moments passed as the staff of the lab waited for confirmation that the older Counselor was alive and well.

The newly awakened giant sat half way up, then dropped back onto the surface of the crate and reached up with both hands and rubbed his face. He grasped the sides of the device with a hand on either side and pulled himself to a sitting position. Karen ordered the door of Kronos' airlock opened. When it swung open he hurried to the Counselor's side. The awakened Counselor stared at Kronos for several moments then reached up and touched him apparently to see if he was really there.

"Kronos?" he said. Kronos grabbed his hand and squeezed it.

"Mentar," Kronos said. Karen and Jean looked at each other.

"Mentar," Jean repeated, "that's his name." Mentar pushed himself up and stepped out of the crate, faltering and then checking his balance. Kronos held his elbow and steadied him. A moment later, they were in each other's arms.

A language exchange began between them. Kronos was talking rapidly with Mentar uttering a word or two now and then. The Counselor finally gestured an apparent 'slow down.' Kronos stacked his hands a foot apart, talking rapidly. Karen and Jean looked at each other surmising that he was telling his Counselor that they, the people of this ship, are small, 'about this tall.' Karen and Jean prepared to step out into the lab and allow Mentar to see them. Security advised caution.

Karen and Jean stepped out into view of Kronos' counselor, now known as Mentar. Kronos touched his arm and pointed. His Counselor followed his gesture. His eyes landed on Karen and Jean. He stared without moving for a long moment. Then he pointed at Karen and Jean and said something to the teen. Kronos turned and looked at his counselor with an open mouth.

"I wonder what he said," Jean said. Karen looked at the translating equipment.

"Just a jumble of words: We...they...saw ... error. The machine can't keep up or cannot understand what they are saying." Karen looked up at Mentar and pointed to the machine. He studied the screen setup then uttered three syllables. Karen quickly studied the screen.

"He's asking how long." Karen looked up, opened her hands, shook her head, then turned to the keyboard and typed: *"Thousands of years."* Then she pointed at the screen. Mentar studied the symbols on the screen for several moments. Suddenly, he straightened up and his eyes went to Karen and Jean. He uttered a phrase with the body language of astonishment, then repeated it. Karen studied the screen. She slowly began to comprehend the meaning. Karen motioned for the Professor to look at the screen then stepped over and activated the intercom.

"Colonel," she said.

"Go ahead, Karen," Marvin said. Karen paused for a long moment.

"The Counselor, the giant, says that we are the 'Little Ones' from the lab. Does that mean what I think it means?" There were moments of silence.

"Apparently," Marvin said slowly, "we are the Cave Men, but thousands of years later."

"It's ironic that we grew up and are rescuing our ancestors," Doug said.

"The ancestors of our intellect," Dave added.

"Colonel," Winston Stone, NASA Administrator, began over the private radio link, "how many can you transport to Earth on Discovery?"

"We've been looking at that, Winston," Marvin replied. "We can take them all in one mission by outfitting Discovery's cargo hold with seating and pressurize it. Since we have only enough gas for four more transfers; perhaps we should get four more of them then return to Earth with the six giants. Then we can prepare to handle the transfer of the rest of them.

"It's a formidable task. Two Guppies running around the clock would take thirty days just to transfer all of them to Discovery."

"That's a long time to be parked on the Moon," Winston said. "Also, think about the logistics of food and other problems. We should do it in maybe four missions. There's also the daunting task of handling all 1,200 at once here on Earth. I like the prospect of three hundred at a time better."

"I do, too," Marvin agreed. "Okay, we'll get three or four more and head home. While Discovery's being outfitted, Karen and her team can better develop communications with the giants. Then, the giants can shepherd the rest of their kind to their new 'home'."

Chapter 21

THE FIVE

George Blevins, the purchasing agent for The National Aeronautics and Space Administration, drove up in front of the aging factory and parked. He stepped out of the car and looked at the front of the fading building. The marquee read: **CUSTOM TARPS, INC.** Underneath the registered company name, already checked out as actually registered and legitimate, read:

Leak Proof Tarps & Lifting Equipment

An older man came out of an open bay door wiping his hands with a shop towel. He had greenish spots on his pants, hands, and one of his cheeks. He turned his head to the side and spat a sizable splat of tobacco juice.

"Could I help ye."

"You are one of the remaining manufacturers of Circus tents?"

"Yep," he said, repositioned his 'chew' then continued: "we make them big enough to hold a whole circus."

"I would like to order some circus tents." The older man spat again the raised his voice:

"Leon, come out here," he said. A younger man appeared at the door, then approached the purchasing agent.

"This guy wants some circus tents."

"We make them," Leon said. "How big you want it?"

"40,000 square feet, an acre, twenty of them." Leon seemed to go into a trance momentarily. Then he turned to the older man.

"Go get Sam." The older man spat again and hurried toward a mobile home parked next to the building. Minutes later a middle-aged brunette, in a pantsuit, pencil behind her ear, and keen eyes approached the buyer.

"Sam, this guy wants some circus tents," Leon said. 'Sam' extended her hand. George took it noticing the strong grip.

"You're Sam?"

"Henrietta; Henrietta Dubois," Sam said. "I don't like Henrietta; I changed it to Sam."

"Well, ah, Sam, we need twenty circus tents, 40,000 square feet in size." Sam paused a moment searching his eyes.

"You're from the government, aren't you?" Sam said. "It's for them giants. You think they'll be trouble?"

"No," George said.

Sam nodded. "Twenty circus tents. That's a lot of money."

"Will fifty-thousand get it started?"

"Yep, that'll do it. Then, I'll bill you as we go."

"How soon can we get the first one?"

Sam studied George's face. "Are some of them giants already here?"

"No, but they will start arriving soon."

"I've got several rolls of canvas in stock to start. I'll need a month—three weeks at least."

The White House

"Mr. President, Montana has lots of room," Foley said then dismissed his own summation on where to put 1,200 brand new, forty-foot-tall, citizens of planet Earth. Walter Howell ignored the statement but used it as a launch pad.

"Senate committees are a favorite sport. Let's let them work on the problem. They can do what they are so good at; talk, until they decide on a permanent location for Giant City. The location has to be chosen with consideration for weather, supply arrangements, utilities, and medical issues. We have no idea how these people are going to react to Earth and all of its 'bugs.' Fortunately, we have time to work on choosing a location. Forgive the expression but, the giants are on 'ice' for the time being."

"Except the five that the Armada is bringing back from the Moon," Foley noted.

"That's actually a break. It's a chance to learn what it's going to take for them to adjust to Earth's gravity and the medical issue of their immune systems. That might be a big problem. I'm sure the Arcology on the Moon was virtually sterile."

"Oh, I doubt that," came from the back of the meeting room. "You see, gentlemen, for plants, food, to grow it takes bacteria, germination, bugs if you will. I'm sure it was cleaner than Earth, bug-wise, but living there would have required a functioning immune system." Walter Howell looked at the NASA researcher and nodded.

"Then maybe they won't have too much trouble here," he said.

"Let's not kid ourselves. They are going to encounter new challenges to their immune systems; probably have colds, maybe flu, and possibly other illnesses.

"For now, we'll house them adjacent to the Aurora facility, a circus tent city, until there's a decision on their permanent location and the place is constructed. What an undertaking; there's been nothing this big since the Manhattan Project."

On the Moon - The Students

Having a limited amount of the Moon Gas, Discovery's crews laboriously retrieved and delivered to the mother ship three more students from the pool of containers; one more male and two females. It would be enough of a sampling of the giants to see what's involved in moving them to Earth. Namely, the concern was the influence of gravity and the issue of their immune systems. As they were awakened Counselor Mentar spent several minutes giving them a brief orientation then introducing them, by name, to the Little Ones. First was the male; Juno, and then the females; Mayan and Noon. When the last female, Noon, saw Karen and Jean she bent forward, put her hands on her knees and spoke a short phrase. Mentar responded. Noon straightened up, cocked her head to the side and smiled.

"I think she just found out who we are," Karen said.

Chapter 22

GRAVITY

"Yes, Mr. President," Winston Stone said. "They will launch tomorrow morning for Earth. The five I told you about will be aboard. They will be here tomorrow afternoon."

"You'll have to rig something temporary; we won't have their 'house' for two more weeks. We arranged additional help to our supplier to speed things up but two weeks is the delivery date."

"There're only five of them. We'll house them in Mr. Gordon's warehouse, Earth Base, for a couple of weeks. We've already seen to the fabrication of their 'furniture' for now; beds, table, and chairs. Also, using the measurements we got earlier for the pressure suits, we manufactured coverall type clothing for them. That will work temporarily until we get a handle on this thing."

"You know, Winston," Walter Howell said, "that they are going to be a major attraction for some time."

"I know. Perhaps you should speak to the nation about giving us some time. We could do a TV special in a couple of days; show the linguists working with them, that kind of thing. We must be able to communicate better. Later we could get them to do a tour once they understand what's going on. It will give the people a chance to meet them; to see them."

"Okay," President Howell said, "I'll speak to the nation."

"For now, we'll secure the place and go from there."

The Moon

Discovery sat in the central crater awaiting the clock to reach the numbers and the Earth and Moon to reach their relative positions designated by the telemetry program. Outside, the surface of the giant mold now showed traces of 'footprints' of the many ships from Earth that had touched down here to organize then proceeded to an objective on the Moon. They had then returned here, more learned, and then launched back home to planet Earth.

All the shuttles were tucked away in their respective bays, moored for the trip home. In the heart of the second deck, in the special lab, four young giants, and their Counselor lay on thick padding and pillows because, after many exchanges on the communication computer, they were asked to. The doctors in attendance had lobbied for this reclined posturing at launch. They were of the opinion that the young people might have a bold opinion of their own physical prowess and when the ship launched at 1*G* they could be needlessly injured. Mentar, in the wisdom of his age, encouraged compliance. After Discovery was underway the giants could sit up, move around, and explore how they would handle the full value of Earth's gravity. Karen and Jean spread padding for themselves to use as a tutorial following the launch of Discovery. They would sit up and then note if the giants did as well, if they were able to do so.

"Attention all personnel," Marvin announced. "Launch in thirty minutes."

The medical team and security personnel at the special lab went on alert hoping for a smooth transition, though abruptly, from lunar gravity to Earth gravity. Within seconds, body weight would be multiplied six times. A considerable challenge to even the strongest.

"Thirty seconds," Marvin reported. "All personnel prepare for launch." Karen and Jean, with the young giants watching, made gestures of spreading out their reclining pads lying down on them. The giants turned on their sides so they could watch them during launch.

"Five, four, three, two, one." Discovery left the lunar surface instantly, the great mass of the

ship providing a few seconds of mercy transitioning from one-sixth-*G* to Earth's value of 1*G*. However, assuredly the full tug of the universal force was there. Karen and Jean watched the giants closely. They tightened their stomach muscles in an ab crunch when Discovery delivered the full tug of gravity. They held the posture for several seconds and then took a couple of breaths.

Karen sat up. Seconds later Kronos, lying on his side, pushed himself up to an almost erect sitting position, holding his posture with both arms, smiled at Karen, and laid back down. The other three attempted the same exercise. Noon, half way up, went backward onto her back and then kicked her legs in an exasperated manner.

"That's it," Karen said. "Get feisty; get on your feet." The female rolled over on her stomach, almost as if she understood, and got to her hands and knees. She breathed for a moment, then lifted herself with one leg and both arms and set her right foot forward under her. A moment later she did the same with her left foot. In a squatting position, she took three sharp breaths, stuck both arms straight out in front of her, rose to her full forty feet of height, and then looked at Karen and Jean. They were clapping and cheering. The giant smiled and sat down on the padding, breathing heavily. Perhaps the tone-of-voice can bridge many thousands of years and vastly different cultures.

The Counselor, Kronos, his buddy Juno, and the second female, Mayan, rolled over and got on their hands and knees and performed the same exercise. Karen and Jean smiled to each other. It would not be long before the guests aboard Discovery would reclaim the strength given to them by birth on Solaris 4.

Chapter 23

ARRIVAL

"A fifty-foot ceiling on this building makes sense now, doesn't it," Isaac said looking around at the huge furnishings. Al nodded, smiling. They felt like toddlers walking around looking at the newly delivered furniture and associated items to Earth Base. All of Frank's equipment formerly housed and used in the warehouse had been moved to a storage facility off the grounds to make room for some 'guests.' These guests would be here for a month or two until tent city, circus tent city, was set up and functioning just across the highway. A place sure to become the number one tourist attraction on planet Earth.

"I feel small," Al said.

Isaac chuckled. "Comparatively speaking Mr. Billington, right now you are about a foot tall."

"What a development," Al said. "Look at all of this; a doll house built by us only the scale is the other way. It's seven times normal size." Al was quiet for a moment. "I J, do you ever think that maybe Research One should have stayed at home in '98?"

Isaac stopped, faced Al quietly for a moment. "No, I don't. I want to know everything there is to know, scary or not. It's all a part of who and what we are. To me, not knowing is cruel."

Onboard Discovery

Karen watched the five giants readjusting their padding on the floor after the four-minute weightless mid-point turnaround of Discovery. They had no problem with the episode. They even toyed with each other, pushing off the walls and gliding across the lab. Apparently they routinely experienced the condition in their world. Interplanetary travel was common, a wonderful premise that, now, with the advent of the new type of propulsion, would be part of life in the Solar System again.

Karen and Jean went to work with the interpreting computer to convey what awaited the five guests less than two and a half hours away. Clothing and a place to live temporarily were waiting for them upon arrival on Earth. A large number of 'Little Ones' will be waiting to see them. No harm. They are now your neighbors.

Karen wasn't sure how much real understanding was getting through the limited medium of information exchange. The appropriate and prudent security forces would be on alert although no problems were expected.

A gooseneck construction bucket, with a greatly enlarged second bucket temporarily attached, was brought in to the landing area to move the five giants from the eighty-foot high second deck guppy bay down to the ground in front of the open bay doors of Earth Base; their temporary home. Karen, Jean, and two security personnel, would ride down with them.

Discovery's arrival itinerary had been arranged by NASA. She would land on her home launching pad. She would undergo a refitting of the cargo hold to accommodate the transfer of the remaining giants from the Moon in four missions. Some four hundred seats with safety straps, appropriately sized for the giants, would be installed. Clothing, coverall type, one size fits all, would be provided for the guests for their trip to Earth; their permanent home for now.

Only the annals of time would know the eventual home of the handsomely sized intelligent beings. How long would it take to rebuild a Solar System destroyed by a storm; a storm of exploratory research gone wrong? The Little Ones would have done their part to save what they could of the civilization involved.

Earth Base

Discovery slowed its descent as the nine landing struts reached for the launching pad. They contacted and then telescoped into themselves to cushion the landing of the mothership on mother Earth. When the pressure was evenly distributed on the landing carriage, Discovery came to rest. An enormous viewing audience on TV and several hundred onlookers allowed into the grounds of Earth Base along with the news media covering the event waited in anticipation for the giants to appear.

The news anchor explained to the crowd in attendance and the viewing audience on TV that the giants were struggling with Earth's strong gravity, having been on the Moon for a time and therefore could not stand for very long.

The five giants followed Karen and Jean to the bay door of the guppy hangar, holding on to girders, railing, and other supports that presented themselves. With considerable effort, they were able to remain on their feet.

The specially-equipped bucket truck designed for high reach was positioned next to the ship under the guppy's hangar bay. The twelve-wheeled-vehicle set its outriggers and then raised the boom and extended it into position at the open hangar bay some eighty feet above the landing pad. The operator carefully 'tagged' the bay entrance. Karen and Jean stepped into the standard bucket then signaled for the giants to enter their special enlarged bucket for the trip to the ground. The crowd began cheering upon seeing Karen and Jean. They looked out across the crowd and waved.

The Counselor reached outside the bay door entrance and grasped the railing of the huge bucket then stuck his head and shoulders outside, visible to the attending crowd. The ohhhhh's and ahhhh's came from the crowd, along with a couple of screams that were quickly muffled. Karen motioned for Mentar, exaggerating the movement, to come on into the bucket. He did so, holding on to the rails around the platform to help support himself, in full view of the observers and then straightened up to his full height. Karen and Jean came up almost to his knee. Karen looked up at him and signaled for him to wave. He raised his enormous hand and arm and waved, looking around at the hundreds of 'Little Ones.'

The other four giants entered the bucket. The females, the last two to enter, waved at the sea of onlookers with clearly feminine movements, drawing a fresh round of applause. All five of the 'new citizens' waved for minutes, smiling. For the first time since they were schooled in the activity, they understood. Perhaps, action...reaction is a galactic thing as well.

The operator of the bucket truck moved the boom away from Discovery and began the descent of the giants and their mentors. He telescoped the boom into itself until the buckets were forty feet above the ground, then lowered the boom slowly until they were sitting on the concrete in front of the bay door of Earth Base.

The giants saw the furnishings inside, constructed in their size. They looked at each other and headed for the dwelling. They stopped at the door, turned and faced the crowd, waving and smiling. The crowd cheered and the warehouse door slowly closed. Five coverall-type garments, fashioned for them, lay on the beds.

A team of linguists, spearheaded by Karen and Jean, set up residence near Earth Base. Their task; develop meaningful spoken communications with the estranged race of a different time. First suggestion from the institute; find out how much we have in common and work from there. Communication gradually grew better and better.

Chapter 24

GIANT CITY

'Sam' Dubois laid the business card on her desk and picked up the phone. She dialed the number and waited. A polished musical voice answered.

"NASA administration, purchasing department, Mr. Blevins' office."

"Let me talk to that fella' that's looking for circus tents."

"Excuse me?" Sam looked at the card again.

"Is George Blevins there?"

"Yes, ma'am, one moment." The purchasing agent came on the line.

"This is George Blevins."

"Those giants are no longer homeless," Sam said. "The first tent is ready, where do you want it delivered?" The purchasing agent explained that the address was a newly established location just allocated by the postal service. The address, where you erect the tent, will be 100 Main Street, Giant City, Illinois.

"Clever," Sam said. "That's not going to be on the map." Blevins gave Sam the address of Earth Base and instructed her that someone would be waiting for her delivery crew and would show them where to set it up.

Discovery's refitting was nearing completion. A stairway, both 'Little One' and giant friendly, was installed to reach from the waking lab to the cargo hold that had been converted to seating for the giants on their transfer to Earth and Giant City. The stairway featured two separate sets of steps; ninety steps or thirty steps depending on where you were from. Portholes, ten feet in diameter, were installed in the outer hull every fifty feet all the way around the ship. The passengers on this deck would not be flying blind.

Discovery would have the necessary accommodations for 300 to 400 giants each mission to transfer them to Earth. Language communications with the five that were acclimating themselves for Earth living were greatly improved.

The interpreting machine was now 'voice' active. Each human or giant could speak into the equipment and the other could understand and respond verbally. Sometimes the query had to be repeated in different word usage but overall the communication was much better.

With the greatly improved communications with the giants NASA technicians arranged a meeting with Mentar and the four students and the linguists from the institute to explore the origin of the 'Moon Gas.' Following a lengthy discourse, Mentar related his and the student's measured knowledge of the chemical. There was only general knowledge circulating through the populace of the lunar Arcology. The lab was a separate science center from the retirement city on the Moon. In the culture of Solaris 4, a planet with one world government, aging was a precious time and treated with great respect. When a citizen reached a certain age, they were transferred to Solaris 3, (Mars), to lessen the force of gravity and its damaging effect; then at a point further in aging, finally to the lunar Arcology, with its half again lower gravity, to finish out their days. Students were rewarded for tending to them, thereby maintaining their quality of life.

Regarding the Moon Gas, the government of Solaris 4 had been in the process of planning and preparing for a journey to the stars. The gas had been manufactured on Solaris 4 and then shipped to the Moon for storage. The gas arrived at the Moon in wax-like cakes ten-by-ten by fifty feet. When unwrapped, the cakes slowly dissolved from a solid to a gas that produced the effect of extended sleep. There were vast underground stores of it on the Moon. A conduit was planted from the storage to the lab for testing for the stellar journey. There had been talk of an interstellar ship of enormous size parked in orbit around Solaris 6, (Saturn). The scientists had been working on developing hyperdimensional energy to power the starship. The Little Ones had also been part of that project. Perhaps more could be learned from the scientific records still on the Moon and on Solaris 3, (Mars). The Arcology on Mars was also a location of a research lab like the one on the Moon and part of the preparations for the stellar voyage were being done there. The scientists had been planning to launch a completely robotic ship to the realm of the stars and have the crew sleep until they arrived. It's ironic that 1,200 giants had slept 50,000 years and gotten nowhere. However, Mentar had voiced, "We are alive thanks to you, the Little Ones, our friends."

Karen and company felt that with the greatly improved language machine they were ready to shepherd the giants to their new home. However, the team of linguists recommended that Mentar the Counselor, be present to make the first contact with the awakened young. The youths that are now living on Earth were followers. They could guide but would not assume authority; a position not yet understood by the linguists and anthropologists. The Counselor would return to the Moon on Discovery to locate the other five Counselors and, when awakened, orient them to what had happened and to the task at hand.

Giant City, as it had been dubbed, was taking shape as the circus tents, modified for this special application, were delivered and erected. Household item suppliers, many of them, had incorporated a new art into their manufacturing: *Seven-times-it*.

There was some concern in the halls of government about having such a great number of youths of their size, disciplined or not, suddenly introduced to a world where their parents and loved ones all had perished many thousands of year ago.

They would have no closure. The immense amount of time had utterly removed everything familiar. Even if they were able to find specific remains; time would have so dealt with them that there would be only a trace that someone was ever there at all.

Would there be isolated incidents of rebellion, or perhaps organized efforts to try to take over and recapture their lifeways? The Counselors working with them, along with Karen, Jean, and the team of linguists saw no evidence of discord. However, a fact that had been pointed out on several occasions was that the 1,200 now on the Moon, sleeping peacefully, had no idea what had happened to their world or what was about to happen to them. But, would they allow themselves to be governed indefinitely? They could easily overpower the 'Little Ones' should they so desire. However, they were now in an epoch in which Earth is a warring planet and therefore has weaponry. Any rebellion by the newcomers could be quickly put down.

If an accord could be maintained a lot could be learned from them and a lot could be taught to them.   Extending a helping hand across millenniums would be a bold venture indeed.

In view of the enormous task of transporting hundreds of the huge containers from the underground tunnel to the lab and on to the pressurized cargo hold the shuttle crews were cross trained to fly the guppies and handle the hardware necessary to complete the task.

The guppies would run around the clock to expedite the transfer of the decided 300 giants per mission. When the other five Counselors were awakened and oriented, two could remain on Earth once they arrived and four could remain on Discovery during all the missions.

The glass containers, when empty, would have to be returned to the tunnel. The enormous weight and bulk of hundreds of them would be prohibitive. It was estimated that each group would require six days to assemble for transport to Earth and Giant City, Illinois. An unloading ramp had to be constructed for the giants to disembark Discovery. Each giant would have a body weight of approximately 1,200 pounds with some ten-to-twenty on the ramp at a time. Fortunately, their living quarters, Giant City, was about a quarter-mile away; not very far when you are forty feet tall. They could walk. With their stride, about sixteen feet, it would only be about 80 steps.

Chapter 25

THE COUNSELORS

Discovery rose majestically from its launching pad, fully laden with special equipment and several tons of extra food, on her journey to awaken and transfer to Earth, 300 new citizens. The fourth deck, the refitted cargo hold, was now known as the 'Land of the Giants.'

The deck currently had two occupants. Mentar had opted to take Kronos with him back to the Moon to transport the first 300 to Earth. There was something significant about that decision that set well with all concerned. After all, Kronos was known to be okay and able-bodied. Also, it indicated that Mentar was applying himself to help make this undertaking work.

Should fate have something wrong with his fellow Counselors, he would have help, though limited, in Kronos. He had been informed about the special pressure suits manufactured in his and Kronos' size. He informed Karen and Jean that he knew where the other Counselors were and that he and Kronos would point out their containers when Discovery arrived and was ready to awaken them.

As Discovery 'steamed' toward the Moon on its fresh and new telemetry flight path, Mentar and

Kronos explored at length the accuracy of the further developed interpreting machine with Karen and Jean. The exchanges became more and more clear. Soon Mentar petitioned Karen and Jean: "Your math does not work."

"What math?" Karen inquired.

"You plan four ships. There's five." Karen and Jean looked at each other, then contacted Marvin. He came to the lab.

"Colonel," Karen said, "Mentar says there are five shiploads of students to go to Earth." Marvin looked up at the Counselor and spread his hands as he had seen Karen and Jean do as a gesture of 'clarify' or 'what do you mean.' The giant said through the machine that there were 400 more students in a different location in the lab. Mentar stated that he would take Discovery's leader to them. With them also were two of his fellow Counselors. Marvin ordered two of the special pressure suits be delivered to the lab so Mentar and Kronos could get familiar with them prior to arriving on the Moon. The burden had just gotten heavier. Marvin notified Winston Stone, who called President Howell, who enlarged the building permit for Giant City.

Moon Base

Marvin steered Discovery to the selected area to receive the first 300 giants for their awakening and transfer to their new home on Earth. The Guppy crews were standing by for immediate dispatch to begin the tedious task of removing the first group of passengers from their silent home to an 'awake' world. The first objective; awaken the five remaining Counselors from Solaris 4 and have Mentar orient them. After all, they would speak Moon fluently.

Marvin, Doug, and crew launched Shuttlecraft One. Frank, Dave, and crew launched Shuttlecraft Two. JD and crew launched Guppy One with Mentar and Kronos in the cargo hold, suited and ready to direct the Armada to the next order of business: the co-Counselors of Mentar. The giant asked to be taken to the location where his container was found. The three ships, lights on, flew directly there. JD touched down and opened the cargo hold and allowed Mentar and Kronos to crawl out of the Guppy's cargo hold and get to their feet.

Mentar went over to the empty space where he had slept for many centuries and then pointed at the next three containers placed in line toward the lab. He held up three fingers.

"Three of them are right here," Marvin said. "Okay, where are the other two?"

Mentar, followed by Kronos walked back to the center aisle and started toward the lab, walking at a brisk pace. The three ships followed, their lights highlighting the giant's movements along the hallway. Their walking among the containers, also giant-sized, gave the appearance of a normal scene.

"These guys are walking at about twenty miles an hour," Doug said. Soon the two giants had walked past the end of the containers and started down the incline where the tunnel enlarged. When they reached the bottom, Mentar suddenly turned to the left with Kronos following closely behind him and went over to the wall, where he turned a corner and disappeared from view. Marvin accelerated Shuttle One to the corner. An entrance going under the tunnel to a second level came into view. Shuttlecraft One entered, followed by Shuttlecraft Two and the Guppy. Mentar and Kronos were waiting. When the Shuttle's lights illuminated the entrance Mentar searched up and down the wall, then, locating it, he stepped on a raised block-shaped extension at the base of the wall. The entire area was flooded with light.

"Well," Marvin said, "looks like our friend knows where all the goodies are." A fifty-foot wide hallway went a hundred yards and then opened into another tunnel the same dimensions as the tunnel above. It came to a dead end less than a mile away. Again, the containers were eight across the tunnel and spaced the same. These containers were mounted on six-foot-high racks with the plumbing to deliver the Moon Gas visible under them. The containers were dust free, protected by their location.

Mentar went directly to the first two containers and looked inside the nearest one. He recoiled, and then looked closer. He straightened up, stuck both arms straight up, fist clenched, and yelled in anguish. He then hit the top of the crate with the sides of his fists. Kronos hurried over and looked into the container. He recoiled and backed away. He was visibly shaken. Mentar looked again inside the container, turned and looked at Shuttle One, and then back at the container. Marvin and crew saw the hurt in his eyes. Marvin eased Shuttle One close to the container and up close to the ceiling and looked down inside the device. They saw the withered remains of a giant, obviously long dead.

Mentar stepped over and checked his other colleague. The same; long dead. He walked along the row of units looking inside. It soon became a fact that this system in this tunnel has failed long ago and all these students had perished in their sleep.

Marvin carefully flew Shuttle One across the spread of glass containers and checked inside them. All gone; no survivors. He did take note that he saw no remains that were contorted or showed any other evidence of pain and suffering when the end came. He hoped Mentar had noted that too, since these were his people and two of them, no doubt, his close friends.

When Marvin returned to the entrance position where Mentar was still standing by his friend's remains, he looked at the giant, gestured toward the sea of containers, and shook his head. Marvin held Mentar's eyes for several moments; something passed between them. Then, Mentar looked down for a moment, then back up and indicated the Guppy's ramp. JD lowered it and Mentar and Kronos climbed into it to be returned to Discovery and duty.

Marvin sensed that Mentar had come to a decision; *save the living 1,200.*

Marvin contacted President Howell and apprised him of the development. Many meetings would follow on the appropriate handling of the matter; seal off the tunnel as a memorial? The giants would be consulted. It would be an opportunity to set a precedent regarding Earth's posture in such matters and to learn the giant's feelings regarding the same.

The two guppies delivered the three Counselors that were sleeping in the main tunnel to the lab in Discovery. With Mentar in the lab-to-ship airlock, maintenance shut off the feeder gas and removed the lids. Mentar entered the lab and waited for his colleagues to awaken.

As they began to stir, he walked from one to the other so they could see him when they became awake and aware of their surroundings. They looked around at length and then at Mentar. When all were fully awake, he spoke. The interpreting machine echoed his words in English. "I want you to meet some friends of mine."

Karen leaned toward Jean. "Looks like their culture incorporates some subtleties too." Karen and Jean stepped out into the open. Mentar gestured in their direction. The three Counselors' eyes followed. They found the two 'one-foot-tall' hosts all at the same time. They stared for moments and then their eyes went to Mentar.

"The Little Ones from the lab. Much time has passed. You are in their spaceship." A storm of words flooded from the three Counselors so fast and grouped that the machine could not keep up. They talked for minutes while Karen and Jean waited, ready to exit quickly if it proved necessary. Minutes later, the group became quiet.

One of the Counselors spoke: "How long?" Karen gestured toward Mentar. He responded with a gesture for all of them to sit down. He joined them on the floor and began a conference that lasted for over an hour. When finished, Karen asked Mentar to conduct a tour of the upper giant's deck so he and his associates could send the awakened youths there when they felt they were settled enough following their awakening.

They would have to be prepared for what they would see upon entering the upper deck. The portholes would be their first look at the ruins of their once fabulous city. The three newly awakened Counselors made the circuit themselves. There was a marked reaction to the, now desolate, condition of their lunar dwelling. The next 300 to be awakened would need to be prepared for what they would see upon entering the cargo deck.

With the 'receiving team' in place, the guppies began bringing the students aboard two at a time. The procedure had been changed to expedite handling. The two guppies would discharge two containers each into the hangar bay and then pick up two empties each and depart. The bay door would be closed, the bay pressurized, then the four moved into the lab. The four students would be awakened. Their Counselors would see that they were oriented and then seated in the lab to await the next four. When the group grew to twelve they were lectured, briefed on needed information and then dispatched to the upper deck.

The giants in the converted cargo hold began growing in numbers as the system began to work smoothly. As the students topped the stairs to the upper deck, the furnishings had a settling effect on them. Upon spotting the portholes they spent their first minutes and, for some, hours going from one to the other.

The crew soon established the frequency of the comings and goings of the two guppies; followed by another twelve coming up the stairs after so many trips by the odd-looking machines. After twelve hours, there were forty-eight on the upper deck. The team shut down operations for a four-hour break; an opportunity to feed the giants and to have a meal and rest themselves.

An extension of the ship's galley had been incorporated into the upper deck. An area, cordoned off from the seating area, was equipped with the necessary equipment for heating and serving soup, bread, and water to the giant youths until they were deposited on Earth, their new home.

Chapter 26

THE STUDENT BODY

Discovery, laden with its first 300 giants and their four Counselors, touched down on its launching pad. The newly fabricated gangway was telescoped into position, ready to disembark the 'Moon' people. They had been laboriously schooled on what to expect upon arrival on Earth. They would leave the ship, descend a special ramp and then follow a marked pathway to their provided dwellings. Each had been provided with clothing in the form of a one-piece coverall-type garment. The first order of business was getting all of their fellow classmates out of perpetual sleep and back to a life.

Discovery was immediately resupplied and serviced. The dedicated crews focused on the missions vigilantly. After a very demanding month, all 1,216 students of 'The University of Solaris 4' were awake and orienting themselves to planet Earth. Their school, the best possible designation in English, was designated by best guess when described by the students themselves as the equivalent of a liberal arts college.

Life now in Giant City, Illinois was about physical conditioning. The students were working toward adapting to Earth's gravity as they were before the 'softening period' they had spent in service on the Moon. Physiologists predicted three months until their general physical condition would be virtually normal.

There was much to be addressed. The newcomers, all but four, were children, more specifically, young adults and did not know about Earth's lifeways, culture, development, and substructure of the society. For example; Earth was wrapped in transmitted electricity; highly energized transmission lines, right out in the open that would strike a fatal blow if touched by one of the teens from Solaris 4. Most of the electric wires were at eye level to them. They could be warned off them, of course, however, accidents would occur.

From the discovery of electricity by man, to its incorporation into everyday use took fifty years. Going from the above ground network to safely underground would take at least the same amount of time.

Additionally, transportation problems had to be addressed. Vehicles could easily be constructed for them; however, the infrastructure would not accommodate them. Bridges, overpasses, tunnels, and again, electric lines crossing the roadways were an unsolvable problem, save society taking a major step forward and moving to flying cars; at least for the giants.

These new residents would be citizens of Earth for the foreseeable future. They would need their hands tied to something constructive. They would need to be incorporated into society and that would require that they be taught to speak English. That would be job-one. Volunteers were recruited to learn 'Moon;' their language. There were a surprising number of applicants; something new and exciting. Life on planet Earth now included citizens forty feet tall.

Epilogue

THE JOURNEY

Maintenance crews, tending Discovery, went about the chore of cleaning the ship in dock. The galley was steamed and restocked. The freezers were kept running with an electrical feed from the dock that also kept the lighting energized and all motorized appointments online. The same maintenance arrangement kept fresh air being constantly circulated through the ship all the time it was docked.

"Next stop, Mars." The maintenance crew stopped and looked at their team member who was vacuum-sweeping the 'land of the giants;' deck four.

"You think so, Will?" He nodded.

"It's inevitable. Once the first step is taken, the journey has begun. Besides, just think what's waiting on Mars. I heard that some of those giants were born there and then moved to Solaris 4."

ABOUT THE AUTHOR

Dan Holt is a U.S. Army veteran, having served three years as a Communications Specialist in Germany. He spent the remainder of his civilian career as a self-taught engineer, designing and testing large-scale production equipment for the file folder industry. The efficiency and durability of his designs even garnered interest from some foreign manufacturers.

In retirement, Dan has used his writing skills to express his continuing fascination with machinery and science fiction. His zest for adventure and intrigue continue to rule in this sequel to UNDERNEATH THE MOON. His variety in sci-fi thought is evident in his second novel, *SLEEP MODE* and in his recently-released fourth novel, KEEPSAKE.

Coming soon: UNDERNEATH THE MOON 3.

See all of Dan's works at the publisher's web site, www.maxholtmedia.com.

www.ingramcontent.com/pod-product-compliance
Lightning Source LLC
Chambersburg PA
CBHW061603170626
46811CB00001B/300